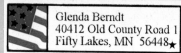

When the Lord leads, Richard leaves behind his prestigous city job. . .

"What?" Sarah's jaw dropped at the incredible news. "A farmer? You are planning to be a farmer?"

Richard didn't flinch. "Yes, I am."

"But you have such a promising future with the captain!"

"Perhaps in a sense, yes. But I'm unhappy in my current position and I've known for quite some time now that it's not for me."

Sarah stood and was thoughtful for several long minutes as she gazed out over the lake. "So what you're telling me is. . .if I marry you, Richard, I will be a farmer's wife."

"That's right."

"No! Never!" Sarah declared, spinning around to face him. "I care for you, Richard, but not *that* much."

ANDREA K. BOESHAAR, who also writes as Andrea Shaar, makes her home in Wisconsin. Her writings reflect her conviction that God is always in control.

Books by Andrea Shaar

HEARTSONG PRESENTS
HP79—An Unwilling Warrior

An Uncertain Heart

Andrea K. Boeshaar

Heartsong Presents

For my mother, Janice Kuhn,
who encouraged me in writing this book
. . .and who hates typing as much as I do.
I love you.

A note from the Author:
I love to hear from my readers! You may write to me at
the following address: **Andrea K. Boeshaar**
Author Relations
P.O. Box 719
Uhrichsville, OH 44683

ISBN 1-55748-919-X

AN UNCERTAIN HEART

Cover illustration by Randy Hamblin.

PRINTED IN THE U.S.A.

one
Milwaukee, Wisconsin
June 1866

Union Depot was a flurry of activity as porters hauled luggage and shouted orders to each other. Reunited families and friends hugged while well-dressed businessmen walked along briskly, wearing serious expressions.

Just outside the train station things were bustling as well, what with all the carriages and horse-pulled streetcars coming and going on Reed Street. Sarah McCabe had all she could do just to stay out of the way. And yet she rejoiced in the discovery that Milwaukee was not the small farm town she'd assumed. In fact, it wasn't all that different from Chicago where she had spent the last nine months teaching music. The only difference she could see right off was that Milwaukee's main streets were cobbled, whereas most of Chicago's were paved with wooden blocks.

Looking down the street now, Sarah squinted into the morning sunshine. She wondered which of the carriages lining the curb belonged to Kyle Sinclair. In his letter, Mr. Sinclair had said he would meet her train. Sarah glanced at her small locket-watch. It was 9:30 and a half hour later than Mr. Sinclair had said he'd meet her. Sarah's train was on time. Had she missed him somehow?

My carriage will be parked along Reed Street, Mr. Sinclair had written in his last letter, the one in which he'd offered Sarah the governess position. *I shall arrive the same time as your train: 9:00 A.M.* The letter had then been signed: *Kyle Sinclair.*

Sarah let out a sigh and tried to imagine just what she would say to Mr. Sinclair when he finally came for her. Then she tried to imagine what the man looked like. *Older. Distinguished.*

5

Balding and round through the middle. Yes, that's what he probably looks like, Sarah decided, and she eyed the crowd, searching for someone who matched the description. Several did, although none of them proved to be Mr. Sinclair. With another sigh, Sarah resigned herself to the waiting.

 za

Last August, Sarah had left her home in rural Missouri for the excitement of the big city: Chicago. As the youngest McCabe, she had grown tired of being pampered and protected by her parents as well as her three older brothers, Benjamin, Jacob, and Luke, and her one older sister, Leah. Sarah thought they all had nearly suffocated her. Oh, they loved her, of course, but Sarah felt restless and longed to be out on her own.

So she'd obtained a position at a fine music academy in Chicago—one of which her parents approved—and began her travels, enjoying every minute of her newly found freedom. She had made good friends in Chicago, friends she was sorry to leave for the summer months. However, the academy was closed during June, July, and August. Therefore, Sarah had been forced to seek other employment for the summer. Either that, or return to Missouri—a fate worse than death as far as Sarah McCabe was concerned!

Then she had seen a newspaper advertisement. A widower by the name of Kyle Sinclair was looking for a governess to care for his four children. Sarah answered the ad, she and Mr. Sinclair corresponded numerous times, she'd obtained permission from her parents—which had taken a heavy amount of persuasion—and then she had accepted the governess position. She didn't have to go home. She would work in Milwaukee for the summer. Another adventure!

Now, if only Mr. Sinclair would arrive.

In his letter of introduction he explained that he owned and operated a business called *Sinclair & Co., Ship-chandlers and Sail-makers.* He had written that it was located on the corner of Water and Erie Streets. Sarah wondered if perhaps Mr. Sinclair had been detained by his business. Next she wondered if she ought to make her way to his company and announce herself, if, indeed, that was the case.

An hour later, Sarah was certain that had to be the case!

Re-entering the depot, she told the baggageman behind the counter that she'd return shortly for her trunk of belongings and, after asking directions, her reticule in hand, Sarah set out for Mr. Sinclair's place of business.

As instructed, she walked down Reed Street (or South Second Street, as it was also called) and crossed a bridge over the Milwaukee River. Then two blocks east and she was on Water Street. From there she continued to walk the distance to Sinclair and Company, which she found with little effort. The building was three stories high, square in shape, and constructed of red brick.

Crossing the busy thoroughfare, which was not cobbled at all but full of mud holes, Sarah lifted her hems and walked up the few stairs leading to the front door. She let herself in and a tiny bell above the door signaled her entrance.

"Over here. What can I do for you?" a young man asked, sounding quite automatic about it, for his gaze hadn't left his ledgers. Sarah noted his neatly parted straight blond hair—as blond as her own—and his round wire spectacles.

Sarah cleared her throat. "Yes, I'm looking for Mr. Sinclair."

The young man looked up now and, seeing Sarah standing before his desk, he immediately removed his spectacles and stood. He was quite tall, she noticed, and he wore a crisp white dress shirt and black tie, although his dress jacket was nowhere in sight and his shirt-sleeves had been rolled to the elbow.

"Forgive me," he said apologetically, looking a bit surprised. "I thought you were one of the regulars. They come in, holler their orders at me, and help themselves."

Sarah gave him a slight smile.

"I'm Richard Navis," he said, extending his hand. "And you are. . ."

"Sarah McCabe," she replied politely as she placed her hand

in his, "formerly of Maplewood, Missouri, but most recently of Chicago."

"I see." Richard grinned in a mischievous way. "A pleasure, Mrs. McCabe."

"Miss," she corrected.

"Ahhh. . ." he said as his deep blue eyes twinkled, "then more's the pleasure, Miss McCabe."

The young man bowed over her hand regally and Sarah yanked it free as he chuckled.

"That was very amusing," she said dryly, for he'd obviously done that on purpose in order to check her marital status. *The cad.* But worse, she'd fallen for it! The oldest trick in the book, according to her three brothers!

Richard chuckled again, but then put on a very business-like demeanor. "And how can I help you, Miss McCabe?" he asked.

"I'm looking for Mr. Sinclair, if you please," Sarah told him, noticing that the young man's dimples had disappeared with his smile.

"You mean the captain? Captain Sinclair?"

"Captain?" Sarah frowned. "Well, I don't know. . ."

"Well, I do," Richard said with a grin, his dimples winking at her now. "He manned a gunboat on the Mississippi during the war and earned his captain's bars. When he returned from service, we all continued to call him Captain out of respect."

"I see," Sarah said, feeling rather bemused. "Then I'm looking for Captain Sinclair, if you please."

"Captain Sinclair is unavailable," Richard stated with a devilish grin. . .as though he'd been leading her on by the nose since she'd walked through the door. "I'm afraid you'll have to do with the likes of me."

Sarah rolled her eyes in exasperation. "Mr. Navis," she began, "you will not do at all. I need to see the captain. It's quite important, I assure you. I wouldn't bother him otherwise."

"Miss McCabe," he countered, "the captain is not here. Now,

how can I help you?"

"You can't!"

The young man raised his brows and looked taken aback by Sarah's sudden tone of impatience, but Sarah didn't care. She crossed her arms and took several deep breaths, wondering what on earth she should do now. She gave it several moments of thought.

"Will the captain be back soon, do you think?" She tried to lighten her voice a bit.

Richard shook his head. "I don't expect him until this evening. He has the day off and took a friend on a lake excursion to Green Bay. However, he usually stops in to check on things, day off or not. . .Miss McCabe? Are you all right? You look absolutely stricken."

Sarah snapped her mouth shut, realizing she'd been fairly gaping. *Mr. Sinclair—that is, the captain—not here?*

Then she reached into the inside pocket of her jacket and pulled out the captain's last letter—the one in which he stated he would meet her train. She looked at the date. . .today's. So it wasn't her that was off, but him!

"It seems that Captain Sinclair has forgotten me," she said, handing the letter to Richard.

He read it and looked up with an expression of deep regret. "It seems you're right."

Folding the letter carefully, he gave it back to Sarah. She accepted it, fretting over her lower lip, wondering what she should do next.

"I'm the captain's steward," Richard offered. "Allow me to fetch a cool glass of water for you while I think of an appropriate solution."

"Thank you," Sarah replied. She felt as though he truly meant to help her now, instead of baiting her as he had before.

Sitting down at a long table by the enormous plate window, Sarah pulled off her gloves and waited for Richard to return.

He's something of a clown, she decided and she couldn't help but compare him to her brother Luke. However, just now, before he'd gone to fetch the water, he had seemed very sweet and thoughtful. . .like Benjamin, her favorite big brother. But Richard's clean-cut, boyish good looks and sun-bronzed complexion. . .now they were definitely like Jacob, her other older brother.

Sarah smiled and let her gaze wander about the shop. She was curious over all the shipping paraphernalia. But before she could really get a good look at the place, Richard returned with two glasses of water. He set one before Sarah, took the other for himself, and then sat down across the table from her.

He took a long drink. "I believe the thing to do," he began, "is to take you to the captain's residence. I know his housekeeper, Gretchen."

Sarah nodded. It seemed the perfect solution.

"I do appreciate it, Mr. Navis, although I hate to pull you away from your work." She gave a concerned glance toward his books, piled upon the desk.

Richard merely chuckled. "Believe it or not, Miss McCabe, you are a godsend. I had just sent a quick dart of a prayer to the Lord, telling Him that I would much rather work outside on this fine day than be trapped in here with my ledgers. And then you walked in." He grinned. "Your predicament, Miss McCabe, will have me working out-of-doors yet!"

Sarah smiled, heartened that he was a believer. "But what will the captain have to say about your abandonment of his books?" she asked in a teasing manner.

Richard shrugged, looking sheepish. "Well, seeing this whole mess is *his* fault, I suspect the captain won't say too much at all."

Sarah laughed, as did Richard. However, when their eyes met . . .sky-blue and sea-blue. . .an uncomfortable silence settled down around them.

Sarah was the first to turn away. She forced herself to look around the shop and then remembered her curiosity. "What exactly do you sell here?" she asked, eager to break the sudden awkwardness.

"Well, exactly," Richard said, looking amused, "we are ship-chandlers and sail-makers and manufacturers of flags, banners, canvas belting, brewers' sacks, paulins of all kinds, waterproof horse and wagon covers, sails, awnings, and tents." He paused for a breath, acting quite dramatic about it, and Sarah laughed. "We are dealers in manilla, hemp and cotton cordage, lath yarns, duck of all widths, oakum, tar, pitch, paints, oars, tackle, and purchase blocks...*exactly!*"

Sarah swallowed her laughter. "That's it?" she asked facetiously. "That's all?"

Richard grinned. "Yes, well," he conceded, "I might have forgotten the glass of water."

Smiling, Sarah took a sip of hers. And in that moment she decided that she knew how to handle the likes of Richard Navis—tease him right back, that's how! After all, she'd had enough practice with her big brothers!

They finished up their cool spring water and then Richard hitched up the captain's horse and buggy. He unrolled his shirtsleeves and, finding his dress jacket, he put it on. Next he let one of the other employees know he was leaving by shouting up a steep flight of stairs, "Hey, there, Joe, I'm leaving for a while! Mind the shop, would you?" Finally, Richard announced he was ready to go.

"Do you know the Lord Jesus, Miss McCabe?" Richard asked after they had picked up her baggage from the train station. They were now heading for the captain's home.

Sarah smiled graciously. "Well, yes, I do. I asked Jesus into my heart when I was just a little girl. Why do you ask?"

"I always ask."

"Good for you!" In his present state, Richard reminded her of Luke. He was a serious Christian, too. "My father is a pastor in

Missouri," Sarah offered, "and two of my three brothers are missionaries out West."

"And the third brother?"

"Benjamin. He's a photographer in St. Louis. He and his wife, Valerie, are expecting their third baby in just a couple of months."

"How nice for them."

Nodding, Sarah felt a blush creep into her cheeks. She really hadn't meant to share such intimacies about her family with a man she'd just met. But he seemed so easy to talk to. Like a friend already. However, Sarah soon recalled her sister Leah's words of advice: "Outgrow your garrulousness, lest you give the impression of a silly schoolgirl! You're a young lady now. A teacher . . ." Sarah promptly remembered herself and held her tongue—until they reached the captain's residence, anyway.

"What a beautiful home!" she exclaimed as Richard helped her down from the buggy.

"Yes, it's quite a sight," he agreed.

Walking toward it, Sarah looked up at the enormous brick mansion. It had three stories of windows which were each trimmed in white, and a "widow's walk" at the very top gave the structure a somewhat square design. The house was situated on a quiet street across from a small park which overlooked Lake Michigan. But it wasn't the view which impressed Sarah. It was the house itself.

As if sensing this, Richard said, "Notice the brick walls which are lavishly ornamented with terra cotta. The porch," he said as they climbed its stairs, "is cased entirely with terra cotta. And these massive front doors are composed of complex oak mill-work, hand-carved details, and wrought iron. The lead glass panels," he informed her as he knocked three times, "hinge inward to allow conversation through the grillwork."

"Goodness!" Sarah breathed, fairly awe-struck. Then she looked at Richard and grinned impishly. "You are something of a walking text book, aren't you?"

Before he could reply, a panel suddenly opened and Sarah found herself looking into the stern countenance of a woman who was perhaps in her late forties.

"Hello, Gretchen," Richard said in a neighborly way.

"Mr. Navis." She gave him a curt nod. "Vhat can I do for you?" Sarah immediately noticed her thick German accent.

"I've brought the captain's new governess," Richard announced. "This is Sarah McCabe." He turned. "Sarah, this is Mrs. Gretchen Schlyterhaus, the captain's housekeeper."

"A pleasure to meet you, Mrs. Schlyterhaus," Sarah said, trying to sound as pleasing as possible, for the woman looked quite annoyed at the moment.

"The captain said nussing about a new governess," she told Richard, fairly ignoring Sarah altogether. "I know nussing about it."

Richard grimaced. "I was afraid of that," he murmured and Sarah gave him a quizzical look. "Let's show her that letter. . .the one from the captain."

Sarah pulled it from her inside pocket, handed it over, and Richard showed Gretchen who, even after listening as Richard read its contents, maintained that she knew "nussing" about a new governess.

Finally she closed the door on the both of them and together they walked back to the carriage.

two

"Now what?" Sarah asked.

Richard helped her climb in. "You'll have to stay with me this afternoon," he stated, looking none too disappointed.

Sarah rolled her eyes.

"We'll have some lunch, I'll show you around town, and—"

"And you won't have to look at your ledgers for the rest of the day," Sarah finished for him with a little laugh.

"My, my, Miss McCabe, you're quite astute," Richard said, climbing into the buggy.

"And you're quite a stinker. I've got an older brother just like you, too. His name is Luke. He can be quite fun. . .unless I get myself into trouble. There's no persuading Luke when I'm in trouble!"

"You? In trouble? I can hardly believe it!" Richard grinned and flicked the reins. The buggy jerked forward. "Is Luke the photographer or the missionary?"

"Missionary. Benjamin is the photographer."

"Oh, yes, that's right." With a sidelong glance in her direction, Richard gave her a "stinker's" grin.

Sarah just shook her head at him.

"Did you say you're from Chicago?"

Sarah nodded. "I've been teaching music there for the past year. I came to Milwaukee because I saw Mr.—I mean, Captain—Sinclair's advertisement for a governess. I needed summer employment, so here I am."

Richard frowned. "The captain knows this is only temporary?"

Sarah nodded.

"Hmmm. . ." Several governesses had come and gone at the

14

Sinclair household, and Richard didn't think the captain wanted someone on a short-term basis. Then, again, he knew the captain was getting desperate.

Richard shrugged his shoulders and smiled. He enjoyed the way Sarah freely chattered about herself and her family, and he wished she'd do it some more.

"Personally," Sarah continued, "I believe that the reason Captain Sinclair agreed to take me on is because I promised to give his children piano lessons at no extra charge." Sarah laughed. "However, I also made it clear that I must be back in Chicago by the first of September."

But more than he liked to listen to her sweet chattering, he liked to tease her—in fact, he liked that most of all!

"Are you saying," Richard began, feigning a shocked expression, "that I have only until the first of September to steal your heart?"

Sarah raised a brow, though she didn't appear shocked by his comment in the least. "Mr. Navis," she replied, "the only Man able to steal my heart thus far has been Jesus, my Savior."

Richard chuckled for a good thirty seconds. *That was a pretty good come-back,* he decided.

Sarah just shook her head. "You remind me of my brother Luke. He teases me incessantly. The day he left to go West was a day to rejoice for me!"

Richard couldn't help grinning at the tart reply and he wondered how many young ladies wished he'd go West on account of his teasing. In fact, he knew of several who would gladly buy his ticket! It truly seemed to him that most women these days didn't have a sense of humor whatsoever—how tragic—except for his mother. Now, there was a woman who appreciated a good laugh!

"I must confess," Sarah was saying, "I do miss Luke now that he's gone. But he's doing very well out there and I believe he'll be back in the fall. He started a church in Arizona—in just a little nothing town. He needs a school teacher and I wanted to be the one; however, my father said it was out of the question."

"Good for your father!" Richard replied earnestly. He had never known a young lady willing to venture West. It was quite a trek and, once over, the conditions were hardly luxurious—especially in the "little nothing towns" of the Arizona Territory. It certainly wasn't a place for sweet Sarah the music teacher, Richard decided.

He drove the buggy to Grand Avenue and they ate at a small establishment by the Milwaukee River. They watched the boats and barges sailing in the sunshine as they ate their food.

"My goodness," Sarah said, realizing she'd behaved "garrulously" again. "I have been talking up a lather, haven't I?"

Richard shrugged. "I don't mind."

"Well, you're very gracious and I'm very rude. Imagine, monopolizing our entire conversation! Please forgive me, Mr. Navis."

Richard chuckled. "You're forgiven. . .and it's Richard. I insist. I equate Mr. Navis with my father." He shook his head. "I only wish Gretchen would call me by my first name. She, however, doesn't feel it's in line with her position—even though she has always been Gretchen to me."

Sarah nodded, thinking it over. "All right, then, Richard. Tell me about yourself." She smiled, looking rather embarrassed now. "I certainly have talked enough about me."

Richard smiled. "Fair enough."

Sitting back in his chair, he began to tell Sarah something of himself. He lived with his parents in their home which was about five miles northwest of the city. He had no siblings to grow up with, just farm animals. He'd completed his education in May of last year, which earned him a certificate in accounting.

"But I hate accounting more than words can tell," he admitted.

"Then why continue to work in that capacity?"

"Because I still owe the captain three more months of service." Richard grinned at Sarah's bemused expression. "Captain Sinclair paid for my education," he told her. "A friend of my father's initially got me the job. . .doing dock work. But as soon as the captain discovered I had a 'talent for figuring,' as he put it, he sent me to school."

"What a wonderful opportunity!" Sarah declared. Then she frowned. "But you hate it! The book work?"

"Yes, I hate it. . .although I'm grateful for the education. Knowledge is never lost. That's the way I see it."

Sarah agreed. "But does the captain know you hate your work?"

"Yes, though he constantly encourages me. I believe he'd like me to stay on after my service is up. . .but that's a decision I'll make when I have to. I'm indentured until the end of August. So for now, I leave my fate in the Lord's hands."

With the meal finished, they walked out of the little eating establishment and went back to the captain's store on Water Street.

"Captain Sinclair will be arriving shortly," Richard promised. "And now I, unfortunately, must get back to my books. I do apologize. . ."

"Please don't." Sarah shook her head. "You've done over and above seeing to me. But can I browse a bit?"

"Most certainly."

Sarah walked up and down the wide aisles of the store. In the back, she discovered the manufacturing part of the business. Upstairs, she soon learned, was the chandlery office; their expertise was in contracting for the shipping and receiving of various goods.

Finally bored with her wandering, Sarah sat down near Richard, promising not to chatter while he was busy at work. He just laughed.

At precisely five-fifteen, Captain Sinclair walked in. He was tall, sun-tanned, and darkly handsome—and looked nothing like the distinguished, heavy-set, older man Sarah had imagined. He had thick, black, curling hair and black eyes. Sarah was fairly mesmerized; she'd never seen a man with black eyes before, nor had she ever seen one so handsome!

"Minding my business, are you, Richard?" the captain asked with a chuckle. He gave a quizzical look in Sarah's direction and then turned back to Richard expectantly.

"Captain, this is Sarah McCabe," Richard said. "I'm afraid she's been waiting for you since early this morning."

The captain froze and his expression registered the shock of his error. "Oh, no. . .it's Wednesday," he said weakly. He narrowed his gaze at Richard. "Why didn't you tell me it was Wednesday?"

"Thought you knew that, sir," Richard stated rather flippantly. "After Tuesday comes Wednesday. . .happens every week."

Sarah had to swallow a giggle as Richard laughed. Then, after throwing Richard an annoyed look, the captain laughed, too.

"Miss McCabe," he began in earnest, "I am terribly sorry about this."

Sarah smiled, feeling suddenly shy in the captain's presence. "It's quite all right," she finally managed to say. "Richard has been a wonderful host."

"Well, good."

Captain Sinclair searched her face, and Sarah thought her knees might buckle under his scrutiny, for she had never met a man quite so handsome as the captain!

Richard cleared his throat. "I took Sarah to your residence, Captain, but there was a problem with Gretchen. . ."

"Hmmm. . ." The captain thought about it for a moment. "Is she acting ferociously again?" He chuckled and, turning to Sarah, he gave her a good-natured wink.

Sarah smiled in response.

Richard, however, didn't seem to notice. "Gretchen was more than ferocious, sir," he continued, "and, apparently, she had no idea that Sarah was arriving today."

"Oh, I'm certain I told her." Looking at Sarah, he said, "I gave Gretchen your name and read your letter of qualifications to her . . ." The captain was momentarily pensive. "Well, no matter. I'll take care of Gretchen when I get home." He smiled at Sarah then, in a way that threatened to stop her heart.

Then suddenly his expression changed to one of irritation. "Oh!" he said, looking at Richard now. "I forgot. I have a dinner engagement tonight." He glanced back at Sarah, considering her at great length. Then he turned and faced Richard once more. "Why don't *you* take Sarah to dinner?" he suggested. "Eat slowly, perhaps take a ride, and I'll make sure Gretchen has Sarah's room prepared by the time you return her to my house later."

Richard appeared to think it over.

"Captain Sinclair," Sarah put in, feeling like a burden that neither man wished to bear, "I really can't impose upon Richard. . . again."

"Well, of course you can," the captain said.

Richard just laughed. "It's quite all right," he told her. "I'd consider it a privilege to take you to dinner, Sarah."

She tried to give him her best smile, but, truth to tell, she was tired. She wanted to change her traveling clothes, and she'd absolutely love a bath!

"And don't worry about transportation home tonight, Richard," the captain said. "You may use my horse and carriage."

"Thank you, sir."

"And put dinner and everything else on my tab."

"As you wish," Richard replied, wearing a mischievous grin.

The captain noticed. "But don't over do it!"

"Not to worry, sir."

Captain Sinclair looked worried nevertheless.

Finally, he turned to Sarah. "I'm terribly sorry about all this, my dear. But tomorrow morning will be soon enough for us to get further acquainted."

She merely nodded. Changing her clothes, taking a bath, and settling in for the night were all but forgotten because, when Captain Sinclair looked at her with his black eyes shining, Sarah completely forgot herself.

"Good!" the captain declared, with a clap of his hands. "Then it's all settled!"

He gave Richard a few more instructions, asked about the day's business, then whistled his way out the door.

After he'd gone, Richard said, "There is a small room upstairs where we keep a cot. You might like to rest a bit and then freshen up or even change your clothes. The room is very private, so you needn't worry, and, seeing as your trunk of belongings is still in back of the buggy. . ."

"Thank you, Richard. You are most thoughtful," Sarah said. And suddenly all seemed right in the world again.

three

Richard and Sarah dined at the Kirby House, a hotel on the corner of Mason and Water Streets. Abner Kirby, Richard said, was the mayor of Milwaukee in 1864. Now, however, he was the owner of a fine hotel and known for his peculiar sense of humor. One suite in the hotel was named "Heaven"—the bridal suite. Another was called "Hell." That room, Richard told Sarah, was usually assigned to "inebriates."

"Oh, my!" Sarah replied, aghast, and Richard chuckled.

Then after dinner, Richard took Sarah for a ride through town, pointing out several sites of interest. He showed her the bridges, many of which were under construction. A flood back in April had washed five of them away in the Milwaukee River. The flood had also caused quite a stir among the "wards" which, Richard explained, were sections of the city—mostly ethnic: Irish, German, Italian, and so forth. However, only memories of the old "bridge wars" surfaced during this time of reconstruction and, thankfully, not the wars themselves.

"Years ago," Richard told Sarah now, "there were terrible fights concerning the location of certain bridges and which roadways would be connected. Those days were known as the 'bridge wars.' "

All Sarah could say was, "Oh." She was interested in the history of this city since it would be her home for the next few months, but she was also amazed at the extent of Richard's knowledge.

He must read an awful lot of boring old history books, she thought. *But he can be very entertaining. . .*

And then, very suddenly, the conversation turned from

informative to personal.

"You're twenty-one years old? I can't believe it!" Richard said with a chuckle.

Sarah shot him a stern look from where she sat next to him in the carriage. "If I hear one old maid comment out of you, Richard Navis, I'll—"

"No, no, Sarah, that's not what I find funny." He gave her a side glance. "What's funny," he said in softer tones, "is that no man has succeeded in marrying you."

"Well, my big brothers think it's a tragedy," she retorted.

Richard laughed at the reply, but then soon grew pensive, thinking everything over. He wondered if she had a love interest back in Missouri. Or maybe Chicago. He wondered if she'd lost a lover, as so many had during the Civil War a few years back. But he found it hard to believe that pretty Sarah McCabe didn't have someone.

Richard cleared his throat. "I realize it's none of my business," he began, "but you, Sarah, are much too pretty to be twenty-one and without a husband."

Sarah stifled a giggle. If she had a nickel for every time she'd heard that "you're much too pretty to be without a husband" line, she would be a very rich woman! And, although hearing the comment had been aggravating at first, Sarah now thought it was quite amusing.

Trying to be serious, she turned to Richard. "You think I need a husband, do you? Are you proposing?"

At that, Richard gasped and sent himself into a fit of coughing. Sarah gave him a few good whacks between the shoulder blades.

"Touché, Sarah!"

His coughing now resolved, Richard had to laugh. *Bested*. And never in all his twenty-three years of life had anyone ever gotten the best of him. Not until he'd met Sarah McCabe.

"I suppose that's what I get for prying into your affairs."

"Oh, that's all right. Actually, I'm rather used to it. I guess it's not very natural for a woman to *choose* to remain unmarried. However, I do. I like my independence."

"Independence, huh?" Richard cocked a brow. "You're not one of those woman suffragettes, are you?"

"Hardly." And then Sarah laughed.

Listening to her, Richard smiled. He liked the sound of Sarah's laughter. If a tickle had a sound, her laughter would be exactly it.

They exchanged several more glib comments. Then, as they turned around and headed toward the captain's residence, they both seemed content to ride in an amicable silence.

"Thank you for a most pleasant evening," Sarah said as they stood on the front porch.

Richard grinned. "It was entirely my pleasure—especially as the captain paid for all of it."

Sarah laughed softly, and Richard chuckled as he banged the large, brass knocker on the front door.

Suddenly Sarah was curious. "With no governess, where have the children been all day? Who has been taking care of them?"

"I believe Captain Sinclair's mother, Mrs. Aurora Reil, or simply Aurora, as she prefers, has the children on Wednesdays. She cared for them today and then, as it usually happens, they'll stay overnight at her house which is about a half hour's drive north of here. Aurora will return them in the morning."

"Oh. Then I take it Wednesdays are to be my day off?"

"Yes, or at least that's how it's been in the past. As for a governess, the last two weeks. . .I believe there have been four."

"Four? You're joking."

Richard pursed his lips, but didn't reply. He hadn't been joking, but he certainly didn't want to discourage Sarah either.

The front door suddenly swung open and Gretchen met them with a frowning countenance.

"Good evening, Gretchen," Richard said cheerfully. "I'm returning the captain's new governess."

The housekeeper replied with an indignant toss of her graying hair, and Sarah shifted uncomfortably.

"I trust Sarah's trunk of belongings has arrived by now," Richard continued, undaunted by Gretchen's scowl. "I sent it on before Sarah and I went to dinner this evening."

"Yes, it arrived," she stated irritably.

"Good. Good."

Richard took a step forward, and Gretchen opened the door to them, albeit reluctantly. Taking hold of Sarah's elbow, Richard ushered her into the foyer ahead of him.

"What a lovely hallway," she stated, looking at the floor made up of various shades of brown terrazzo. Then she glanced at the goldenrod, papered walls. "How absolutely lovely."

Gretchen merely donned a bored expression as she lit another lamp and set it upon a marble-top table. "Your room is on the second floor," she told Sarah. "Next to the nursery vhich is in the far hallvay, first door to the right vhen you come up the back stairs. . .and that's another thing: Be sure you use the servants' stairvell and not this vun," She nodded her head, indicating the grand, curving staircase at the end of the foyer.

When Gretchen was out of earshot, Richard said, "Listen, Sarah, if something doesn't seem right. . ." He paused as if groping for words. "Well, please let me know if you're uncomfortable in any way."

"Thank you, Richard, but—"

"Anything at all, Sarah, I mean it."

She smiled, though she was taken aback by his vehemence. "Well, all right. And, thank you again, Richard. For everything."

His expression relaxed and he nodded. "Good night."

Walking behind Richard, she watched him leave and closed the front door after him.

She turned. *Now to finally get myself settled!* she thought.

Taking the lamp which Gretchen had set on the table, Sarah walked through the foyer to the kitchen. It was a large room, tiled white and yellow and scrubbed clean for the night. There appeared to be a breakfast nook at one end of the room, and Sarah noted the children's chairs pushed in around the table.

This must be where the children dine, she thought with a smile. She was counting the hours till their meeting.

And she absolutely loved this house! Why, it seemed like the very house in which she had always dreamed of living, with beautiful rooms and beautiful things. This house was nothing like the small, wood-framed house in which she'd grown up. Three small bedrooms for two parents and five children—Sarah had always felt crowded in her family home. But one could never feel crowded in a home of this magnitude!

Beyond the kitchen was another hallway, dark and imposing. Sarah realized this was the "servants' stairwell." Climbing the steps, she reached the second floor and found her bedroom. She fairly gaped at the sight and, for a moment, she thought she had made a mistake. Such a lovely and spacious chamber for a governess? But, it must be. . .she'd entered the first door to her right, just as Mrs. Schlyterhaus had said. This was it.

Setting the lamp upon a desk in the far corner, Sarah did as much exploring as possible, given the poor lighting. Afterward, she felt one thing was sure: She was going to enjoy living in this home for the summer!

❧

"Good heavens, Richard! Where have you been? I've been worried sick!"

Standing in the kitchen of the farmhouse, the farmhouse which his father had built some fifteen years ago, Richard grinned as his mother came toward him. Her thick auburn hair was tied in rags for the night and traces of cold cream could be seen like patches on her face, while her white cotton nightgown billowed around her ankles as she moved.

"Mama, you're a vision of loveliness," Richard crooned.

Beatrice Navis stopped short, sensing that she was about to be the object of a joke. "The Lord commands that you respect your mother. . .even when she's not at her best!" she retorted.

Richard chuckled nevertheless as Bea smoothed the cream on her face and patted her hair.

"Well, I suppose I do look a sight, don't I?" she admitted.

"A sight for sore eyes, Mama," Richard said with a teasing gleam in his eyes.

"Oh, you just hush!" Bea told him.

Richard laughed and Bea shook her head at him. "You are so much like your father," she said. "Always finding something funny in every situation. Sometimes I truly wonder if I'm the only one in this house with any lick of sense."

Richard shrugged. "Well, I know you love Pops and me anyhow, Mama."

"I do. So where were you tonight, Richard?" she asked again. "I've been concerned."

"I'm sorry," he said sincerely. "Captain Sinclair's governess arrived today and, of course, he forgot about her."

"Is the governess for him or the children?" Bea asked tartly, fully aware of the captain's absent-mindedness.

Richard chuckled. "As far as I know, she came for the children."

"That man needs a wife."

"Well, all he's got is a governess at this point. . .and quite a pretty one, I might add."

Suddenly Bea seemed very attentive. "Is that so? She's pretty?"

Richard nodded. "And I took her to dinner on the captain's orders. We had a very nice time."

Richard knew his mother was eating every word. She'd love nothing better than for her only son to settle down with a pretty wife and produce some grandchildren. So he decided to have a little fun with her.

"We get along very well, Mama," Richard said with a grin. "Did I say she was pretty?"

"Yes. . .yes, you did."

"And she's a believer."

Bea was delighted.

"Her father is a preacher in Missouri, and Sarah teaches music in Chicago. She's only in Milwaukee for the summer."

"And you like her, huh?"

"Oh, yes," Richard replied, fighting to keep a straight face. "Such a pity she's as wide as a house, though." He shook his head, feigning a look of remorse.

In truth, Sarah had a very comely figure, but Richard couldn't resist the prank on his mother.

"Mama, you should have seen her putting the food away at the dinner table tonight. She would have shamed any lumberjack!"

Bea paled beneath her patches of cold cream. "Heaven above!"

"Yes, it is," Richard said with a mischievous grin. He kissed his mother's petal-soft cheek. "And I'm teasing you. Sarah isn't really as wide as a house."

"Richard Andrew Navis!"

"But she is ninety-four. I don't know how she'll ever keep up with those children! However, she uses a cane. . .I suppose that will come in handy."

Beatrice gave her son a level look. "You have five seconds to get up to your bedroom before I thrash you within an inch of your life!"

Richard's eyes widened in mock terror and, taking the steps up two-by-two, he laughed.

four

Sarah awoke early and had her prayer time. Then she washed and dressed in a blue and white striped dress with white apron. For working, she thought the apron was perfect, for a governess or a music teacher both, because it sported two large pockets in the front and it fit nicely over the crinoline underneath the skirt. Moreover, the apron protected her dress. How glad she was that her mother had suggested making several of the aprons.

With a final pat of inspection to her braided and coiled blond hair, Sarah entered the kitchen. Fearing she would encounter Gretchen, she was pleasantly surprised to have the cook, a plump, smiling, talkative woman, seat her at the table and serve her breakfast.

"I'm Isabelle," she told Sarah. "I take care of the cooking, but I leave for my own home at three o'clock or so. Don't board here in the house like Gretchen. And I've got dinner started here by the time I go. Just needs to be served and Gretchen takes care of that."

"I see," Sarah replied. Then she forked another bite of hot cakes and syrup into her mouth. "This is delicious, Isabelle."

The cook smiled with satisfaction and went back to her work at the stove. Sarah finished eating and then walked around the house, awaiting the captain's presence. Unfortunately, it was the children who showed up first. Any introductions and explanations, Sarah realized, were mere wishes at this point; she was left on her own. . .again.

"Well, well, well, who have we here?" asked the beautiful woman accompanying the children. As she bore a decided resemblance to the captain, except for a lighter complexion, Sarah assumed this must be his sister.

Smiling, silently praying in an effort to overcome her nervousness, Sarah introduced herself.

"I'm Aurora Reil," the woman replied. "And these," she said, her gloved hands indicating the children, "are my. . .my. . .my—"

"Grandchildren," put in the tallest and obviously the oldest of them. Then he looked to Sarah with a frown. "Aurora hates the words 'grandmother' and 'grandchildren.' "

"Oh, Gabriel, I don't *hate* them," she replied. "At least not always. I only hate those words when they apply to me."

Sarah was taken aback by the remark. However, when Aurora laughed, Sarah could only wonder if she'd been joking all along. Every grandmother Sarah had ever known wore the title proudly, feeling truly blessed by her grandchildren. Wasn't this grandmother the same?

"I must be off," Aurora declared dramatically. Her chestnut-brown hair was pulled up and pinned in an elegant chignon, and she wore a lovely hunter-green felt hat which matched the silk of her skirt.

Because of the woman's attire, Sarah wondered if she were "off" to an important affair. But then Aurora stated that she was going home to rest after her "duty day" with the children and Sarah had to wonder. Back in Missouri they called dressing up like that their "Sunday-go-to-meetin' best." And here it was only Thursday! Sarah was in awe.

"Ta, ta, my darlings," Aurora said, allowing each child to place a perfunctory kiss on her smooth, powdered cheek. "Be kind to your new governess and I shall see you next duty day!"

With that, she was gone, the great front door closing with finality behind her.

In the foyer, Sarah surveyed the children. Four of them. Two boys—the older ones—and two little girls. Oddly, they didn't look the least bit upset to have been left by their grandmother. And left with a complete stranger, at that! Not even the youngest, who didn't look any older than three years old, seemed tearful.

"Come," Sarah told them, leading the way into the magnificent reception parlor. "Let's get acquainted."

The children followed, albeit reluctantly. Sarah sat down and smoothed out her skirts; however, the children continued to stand and Sarah wondered why.

"Well, I'm Gabriel," the oldest boy offered. "And we're not allowed to sit on the furniture in here," he announced as if divining Sarah's thoughts.

"But sometimes we did anyway," said the older of the two girls, "when Mama was alive."

"Oh, you poor, dear child," Sarah said sympathetically. But as she considered each young face standing before her, she saw all dry eyes and very little emotion.

Curious, she thought. She cleared her throat. "How long ago did your mama die?" She figured it was a long time passing—so long the children could barely remember her.

"Uhm. . .it was a while ago," Gabriel answered in a nonchalant tone.

Still curious, Sarah wondered how long "a while" was, but she decided not to ask.

Then the little girl beside her offered the information. "Our mama died at Easter time, but she was terrible sick ever since Rachel was born."

"You mean 'terribly sick,' " Sarah corrected. "And I'm sorry to hear that." She immediately assumed "Rachel" was the one on her knee.

Turning back to the young girl who had spoken, Sarah searched her eyes. They were like her father's, black as coal. Her features resembled his as well, especially the color of her black hair which hung in one fat braid down her back. So like the captain's, so black the hair looked blue.

"What's your name?" Sarah asked gently.

"Libby," the girl replied.

"Her given name is Elizabeth."

Sarah looked at Gabriel, nodding her thanks for his input.

"And that's Rachel," he said, pointing to the little one now snuggled deeply into Sarah's lap. "He's Michael, my brother." Then, as if to prove the point, the older gave the younger a brotherly shove. "And I'm Gabriel," he said at last.

Sarah studied him with a smile. He was fairer than the captain, similar in coloring to his grandmother. His eyes were hazel and his hair dark brown. The other children, except for Libby, were of the same skin tones, although Michael's eyes were dark brown like his hair.

"How old are you, Gabriel?"

"Twelve. . .and I don't need a governess, either!" he said, looking quite resentful.

"I'm sure that's right," Sarah replied. "Twelve years old is quite mature. However, I've never been to Milwaukee before and I'm going to need you, Gabriel, to show me around the city. Why, I'm also going to need you to let me know how things are done around here at home. Would you help me?"

He shrugged. "I suppose."

"I'll help you, too, Miss. . .Miss. . ."

"McCabe," Sarah offered. "My name is Sarah McCabe, but you can call me Miss Sarah."

"Well, then, I'll help you, Miss Sarah," Michael said with a wide grin. "I'm eleven, but I know more than Gabe does anyway."

"You do not!"

"Do so!"

"Do not!"

"Boys! Boys! Boys!" Sarah exclaimed while trying to hide a smile. "I'm quite sure I'll need both of you," she added diplomatically. "Gabriel? Michael? Is the matter settled?"

Gabriel shrugged and Michael nodded while Libby said that she'd like to help "Miss Sarah" too.

"You can't," Gabriel told his little sister. "You're just a baby."

"I am not! I'm six!" Libby retorted. "Rachel is the baby, Aurora even said so!"

"Really, Libby," Sarah said with furrowed brows, "you don't actually call your grandmother by her given name, do you?"

"If we call her 'Grandmother,'" Gabriel said in a matter-of-fact tone of voice, "she'll throttle us!"

Sarah could hardly believe it, but all of the children were nodding.

"Do you have a grandmother?" Libby asked, leaning closer to Sarah now.

"Well, yes I do and I call her 'Granny.'"

"You do?"

Sarah nodded.

"I think Aurora would kill us if we called her 'Granny,'" said Michael. Then he and Gabriel snickered together over the thought. It was the first time Sarah had seen Gabriel's expression change all morning.

"Well, I see you children are getting along with your new governess."

Sarah turned suddenly at the sound of the male voice coming from over her shoulder. She found Richard standing there, wearing a huge grin.

"Mr. Navis!" The children cried happily and in unison. Even little Rachel squirmed off Sarah's lap to greet him.

Richard rewarded her with a candy stick and then proceeded to treat the other children. He had brought one for Sarah, too, which made her smile.

"What do we say to Mr. Navis, children?" she prompted.

"Thank you!" they answered at once.

Sarah led the children outside where they sat on the front stoop and ate their candy. Sarah, however, pocketed hers for later.

Standing on the porch, Richard told her the captain had sent him. Captain Sinclair had had an early appointment but would be home at lunchtime to give her a bit of orientation.

"The captain sends his apologies."

"It couldn't be helped," Sarah replied, her feelings teetering between disappointment and frustration. Seeing the captain again would be something of a thrill, for she had never met a man so captivatingly handsome. And yet, handsome or not, she simply *had* to see him—to speak with him. It was disturbing to be on her own with these children and to be unaware of what their father expected.

"It would seem you have everything under control," Richard stated.

Sarah smiled, watching the children as they enjoyed the candy. She looked up into the sunshine, now well above the lake.

"And it would seem you, Richard Navis," she said pointedly, "have gotten away from your books and out-of-doors once more."

"Hmmm. . ." Richard made like he had to think about it. "Well, what do you know? I did get away, didn't I?"

He laughed while Sarah shook her head at him.

Then, on a more serious note, he said, "There's a concert tomorrow night at the Shubert Theatre, also known as the Academy of Music. It opened last year and it's quite a popular place. Would you like to go?"

"I. . .I. . .don't know. . ."

"We will be well chaperoned," he added quickly. "I had originally made plans to attend the concert with a group of my friends from church."

"*You* have friends, Richard?" Sarah asked impishly.

Richard answered with an indignant "Humpf!" However, he obviously enjoyed the teasing. Sarah could tell; his eyes were smiling.

Then, feigning a lofty brow, he declared, "Just for that, I shall arrive at precisely seven o'clock tomorrow evening and I will not tolerate any tardiness, Sarah McCabe!"

Richard bounded down the brick stairs, wishing the children a good day. Then, unhitching his horse, he mounted, gave Sarah a grand salute, and rode off, back to the captain's shipping business, and back to his books.

five

Captain Sinclair arrived just before noon, and Sarah and the children joined him in the dining room for lunch. Isabelle had prepared plates of sliced beef and cheese which were served on chunks of freshly baked bread. Then, for dessert, she brought out a jar of her "famous" canned pears. The children, particularly the boys, ate so fast and so much that Sarah wondered if they'd ever be filled. But then, at last, they were.

After lunch, the captain summoned Gretchen and asked her to watch the children while he and Sarah held a brief meeting in his study. Gretchen agreed, but not without sending Sarah a scathing look. Once more Sarah wondered why she was the recipient of such contempt. Was Mrs. Schlyterhaus unhappy in her position? And what did she, Sarah, have to do with it?

"Sit down, my dear," the captain told Sarah after they'd entered his study.

She chose one of the two black leather chairs situated in front of the captain's large oak desk. Nervously taking her place, Sarah nearly jumped out of her skin when the captain closed the door to his study.

"Relax, Sarah," he crooned with a chuckle. "Do you think I'll bite?"

"No. . .no, of course not," she replied, although she wished she could sound more convincing. What was wrong with her anyway? Ever since Captain Sinclair came home for lunch, Sarah had felt awkward and unsure of herself. Then, to further her discomfort, the captain took the chair beside her instead of sitting behind his desk as she'd expected.

"Now, about the children and the household situation as

a whole. . ."

Sarah watched as the captain stretched out his long legs. Tapered black pants were tucked snugly into black boots. His tall frame looked as though it had been poured into the chair, for he seemed so relaxed. Sarah thought it was unfair that he should be so comfortable while she was so nervous!

"As you know from our correspondence," Captain Sinclair continued, "I am a widower. My wife, Louisa, died just over three months ago. She was very sick for a very long time." He sighed. "Her death was almost a relief."

"I see," Sarah said, noting the same dispassionate expression on the captain that she'd seen on his children's faces earlier.

"The children saw Louisa very seldom. So did I, for that matter," he added on a sarcastic note. "She was very beautiful and very. . .busy with her social schedule, as much as her health allowed."

Sarah hid her shock and surprise by lowering her head and momentarily studying her folded hands.

"Louisa and my mother were the best of friends, despite their age difference. They shared a kindred spirit, I suppose." The captain paused, thinking. "Did you meet Aurora this morning, Sarah?"

She nodded. "I must admit, I was a bit surprised that the children addressed their grandmother by her first name. It seems. . ." She caught herself before she used the word "disrespectful." That might be too strong. Clearing her throat, she said, "Well, I guess it doesn't seem conventional, that's all."

Captain Sinclair chuckled. "There isn't anything *conventional* about Aurora. And Louisa was the same way."

Sarah's eyes widened. "Did the children call their mother by her first name also?"

"No, no. Only Aurora gets away with that offense, as it were."

Again he paused and it seemed as if he were debating whether to continue—as if he were debating whether to let Sarah in on some great secret. Finally he said, "It's my intent that my children have some sense of family unity. I never did. Aurora acted more like my sibling than my mother, a fact which she freely admits. A fact of which she seems most proud."

Sarah lowered her eyes once more, this time staring at the plush imported carpet. Her heart was suddenly burdened for the captain and his children.

"I will do whatever I can to further your intent, Captain," she told him, looking up at him now.

"I know you will, Sarah. From your letters, I had a feeling you were both caring and competent."

"Thank you, sir."

The captain went on to describe the past for Sarah so she would fully understand the situation.

"We have had governesses come and go in the last years. I can't understand it, either. No one will stay. I suppose it's our lifestyles . . .that is, Louisa's and mine. When she was alive neither one of us was here very much. Too big of a load for a mere governess to bear, am I right?"

Sarah shrugged helplessly. She thought the problem might have more to do with a certain housekeeper's "ferociousness" than the children being too big of a load.

"The only one of my staff who has stayed on is Gretchen," the captain continued. "She and her husband had been in service with my in-laws—both of whom are dead now, along with Gretchen's husband. But back fifteen years, upon my marriage to Louisa, I acquired both Gretchen and Ernest as household help. Gretchen has been faithful ever since." The captain grinned sardonically. "Of course, I do pay her very well to stay and put up with all of us."

Sarah just nodded.

Then Captain Sinclair went on to give Sarah a few instructions, none of which were beyond reason. Her evenings were her own and Wednesday was to be her day off. She would earn five dollars a week and Sarah nearly gasped at the gracious allotment. Her teaching position in Chicago paid less than that!

"You see," he said, leaning toward her now, "I'm hoping to convince you to stay longer than the summer."

Before Sarah could even think how to respond, the captain asked, "Is everything to your satisfaction? Your accommodations? Your salary? And how about the children? Isn't Rachel a darling?"

Sarah smiled. "Oh, yes, she certainly is."

Just then a knock sounded on the door, and on the captain's, "Come in," Gretchen appeared.

"Mr. Navis has sent a message: You are late for your two o'clock appointment."

The captain frowned. "Did I have a two o'clock appointment?"

Gretchen shrugged. "Apparently."

The captain sighed and looked at Sarah. "It's a good thing I have Richard and Gretchen. . .and now you to look after me."

As he left the room, Sarah furrowed her brows, wondering whose governess he really intended her to be. . .

❧

Richard awoke at dawn. He dressed and took to the stairs. In the kitchen, his mother was cooking breakfast.

"Your father couldn't wait for you this morning," she said over her shoulder while stirring the mixture on the stove. "He's already out in the barn. But even though you're late this morning, don't take it to heart, dear. Your father was up early anyway. His legs. . ."

Bea didn't say anymore. She didn't have to. Richard understood.

Opening the back door, Richard left the family's large kitchen and walked down the wooden ramp which had been built after his father's return from the war. Martin Navis had been wounded in battle. A Rebel's bullet had caught him in the back and the damage caused by removing it had rendered his legs useless. He rode about the house and property in a wooden chair that had two large wheels on each side. Richard had been able to obtain the chair for his father at a good price, too, thanks to Captain Sinclair and all his contacts. And, although his father was confined to the thing, Marty Navis' disposition was as good-natured as the day he'd left for war.

" 'Mornin', Pops," Richard said as he entered the barn. Then he grabbed a pail and proceeded to milk Lyla, one of the family's Guernsey cows.

Marty wheeled up beside him. "I've milked two cows already."

"Sorry, I'm late, Pops. I overslept."

"You overslept by a half hour. Been keeping late hours, there, haven't you, son?"

Richard grinned and then shrugged. "Business is booming."

"Right-o," his father replied, albeit on a sarcastic note. " 'Course I don't imagine your coming in after dark has anything to do with this new governess your mother has been telling me about."

Richard didn't answer right away. Embarrassment got ahold of his tongue. His father's comment was only half-true, however. The captain had been keeping him very busy at the store.

"Sarah has only been in Milwaukee for two days—"

"And you've been seeing to her comfort."

"Yes. . .I mean, no. . .I mean. . ." Richard groped for words. "What I mean is, I've been helping her out because the captain is gone a lot. I haven't been making a pest of myself."

Marty just laughed. "Son, I'm proud of you for taking care of things for the captain like you do. You're a good boy."

Richard chuckled, too. "Thanks, Pops."

And nothing more was said as both men went about their early morning chores. Then, being late as he was, Richard went upstairs, washed and changed into a fresh shirt, donned his tie, grabbed his suit coat, ran back downstairs, gobbled his breakfast—much to his mother's consternation—and then saddled his horse.

"I'm staying at Aunt Ruth and Uncle Jesse's tonight," he told his father as he climbed onto his horse. "I won't see you until tomorrow night."

"Ah, yes, it's Friday," Marty said with a nod of understanding. "Don't suppose you've invited your Sarah to the theater with your church friends."

Richard had to chuckle. "Pops, you've got it over on me."

"Well, I was young once, too, you know."

Then, as Richard was about to ride away, his mother beckoned to him from the back door.

"Ask Sarah to church on Sunday," she called, "and Sunday dinner. The Staffords are coming, too."

Richard swallowed the reply that both his parents were getting more serious about Sarah than he was. But the truth in his heart ran contrary to that. He felt for Sarah more than he had felt for any young lady he'd ever known. She was different in a refreshing sort of way—in a way that made him long to be around her.

"Sarah will most likely have the captain's brood with her," he warned his mother. "Four pistols, you know."

"Oh, I just love those children," Bea said with a sparkle in her eye. "Tell Sarah to bring them. They're invited, too."

"Orders from Headquarters," Marty said with a laugh.

With a wide grin at his father's remark, Richard bade his parents good-bye and rode the three miles into the city to the captain's store on Water Street.

six

On her third day in Milwaukee, Sarah took a walk in the warm summer air while the children ate breakfast with their father. As much as he was not a family man, Sarah thought that he was certainly trying. And his children seemed to adore him, especially the little girls. *Better to give them some time together,* she decided as she slowed her pace. A cool breeze was blowing off the lake and, taking the stairs down to the beach, Sarah walked for over a half hour.

When she finally arrived back at the Sinclair residence, the captain was just getting ready to leave for the day.

"Good morning, Sarah. Out for some air?"

"Yes, Captain. It seemed to get my blood moving."

He smiled. "The lake breezes do that for a body, yes." His smile grew. "So what are your plans for today?"

"We're going fishing!" Gabriel exclaimed, joining in the conversation. "Miss Sarah says she knows how to bait a hook just the way the fish like it."

Sarah grew embarrassed. While the boy meant it as a compliment, Sarah didn't want the captain to think she wasn't lady-like.

The captain, however, didn't seem to notice. "I take it we'll have fish for dinner this evening."

"Oh, you bet we will!" Michael declared while Gabriel nodded.

Libby wrinkled her little nose. "I hate to fish. They smell!"

"I wholeheartedly agree!" Sarah replied. "But I thought you and Rachel could collect precious stones while the boys fish. I have an idea for a special project and it will take lots of beautiful stones and paste."

"Goody!" Libby cried, dancing around her father's knees.

Captain Sinclair laughed. "You'll have fun today. I promise."

He kissed his children good-bye and then waved to Sarah. She smiled and wished him a good day as he left the house.

An hour later, Sarah was back down at the beach, but with the children this time. Libby and Rachel had taken off their shoes and stockings and now had their skirts hiked to their knees as they searched for "diamond rocks." Each girl carried a pail and they walked through the wet sand at the water's edge, looking quite serious about their work.

Sarah sat on the long brick pier, showing the boys how to bait a hook. "You've got to fold up the worm onto the hook. . .like so."

Gabriel was fascinated. "I never knew a lady that wasn't ascared of worms."

"Afraid, Gabriel," Sarah corrected. "And, no, I'm not afraid of worms."

"How 'bout snakes?" Michael asked.

"What kind of snakes?" she countered.

"All kinds. . .but mostly really slimy, slithery ones."

"Oh, those are the best kind," Sarah said, fighting the urge to giggle. No doubt these two stinkers were up to something, what with all their questions.

"Our last governess didn't like any kind of snakes," Michael stated candidly. "She especially didn't like them in her bed."

Sarah gasped. "Mercy! You little rascal! You didn't really put a snake in your last governess's bed, did you?"

"Nope. Gabe did it."

"Gabriel!"

"We didn't like her," he said simply, as if that was all the reason he needed to do such a dastardly deed.

"For shame," Sarah admonished him.

"Well, she was mean," Gabriel said.

"But don't worry," Michael added with his heart in his eyes, "we like you, Miss Sarah. You're not mean. Right, Gabe?"

Gabriel shrugged and Sarah took that as an affirmative, coming from him.

"Well, I'm very fond of both you boys," she told them honestly. "Now, let's get busy and catch some fish!"

❧

Richard couldn't resist. When Captain Sinclair announced that Sarah had taken the boys fishing, he just had to see it. Sarah, the sweet music teacher from sophisticated Chicago, was fishing? That would be a sight to behold for sure!

He balanced the morning's figures, then, just to get out of the store, he volunteered to run the day's errands. After the errands were done, he headed straight for the beach. And there she was. . . bare feet dangling in the water, her blond hair tousled by the lake breeze, her bonnet blown backwards, and a fishing pole in hand.

"If I hadn't seen it, I never would have believed it," he mumbled to himself. Then he chuckled as he walked toward the pier.

"Hi, Mr. Navis," Libby shouted from several feet away.

"Good morning, ladies," Richard called back to Libby and her sister.

"Hey, Mr. Navis!" Gabriel called.

Sarah gasped and spun around. "What are you doing here?" she asked with wide and guilty eyes.

Richard thought she looked as though she'd just been caught in some scandalous act—probably because of her lack of attire. However, having her shoes and stockings off was hardly scandalous, considering this part of the beach was seldom occupied. Most people opted for the public beach closer to the busier section of the city.

He grinned. "I came to see the refined music teacher fishing like an old seaman."

Sarah gave him a quelling look. "Oh, fine. Well, now you've seen me, so go on back to your books where you belong."

Richard laughed.

"And I'm hardly an 'old seaman.'"

"I'll say. But if you're not careful, you'll have a fine sunburn."

Sarah gasped again, and nearly lost her pole to Lake Michigan as her hands leapt to secure her bonnet on top of her head. Richard chuckled all the while.

"Why can't Miss Sarah get a sunburn?" Michael wanted to know.

"Because it will smart," Richard replied.

"More so because it will tan and then I'll look like the farmer's daughter," Sarah said, already worrying that her face and hands would be brown from this outing. How uncouth she would seem to the captain.

"What's so bad about looking like the farmer's daughter?" Gabriel asked, turning away from his fishing pole to look at Sarah.

"Yeah, what's so bad about it?" Richard added. After all, he had been born and raised on a farm. His mother never complained about the sun tanning her skin, and she looked healthy with that little bit of brown.

"A *real* lady," Sarah began, "shades her skin from the sun. In Chicago, all the women whiten their skin with powder. It's stylish."

"So, what you're saying," Richard said, "is that sophisticated city women think it's stylish to look sickly."

"Like Aurora," Michael said, looking proud of himself because he thought he understood.

"And Mrs. Craighue," Gabriel interjected.

"Who is Mrs. Craighue?" Sarah asked.

"She's one of the ladies who visits Father sometimes. She has white skin like you said and wears her dresses so low you can see clear down to her—"

"That's quite enough, Gabriel, thank you!"

Sarah turned a shocked expression on Richard who had the good sense not to laugh but changed the subject instead.

"How many fish have ye caught, men?" he asked, imitating a rugged sea-faring man.

Sarah gave him a warning look for including her as one of the "men."

"We caught three, mate," said Michael, playing his part. "But

Miss Sarah is the one who caught 'em so I guess they don't count."

"Now, see here!" she cried indignantly.

"Besides, they're puny," Gabriel added.

Sarah clicked her tongue derisively. "That does it! I'm going to help Libby and Rachel collect diamond rocks!"

Richard laughed and laughed. What fun she was!

"You're not *really* angry, are you, Miss Sarah?" Michael asked.

"You bet I am!"

But then she turned and gave the boy her sweetest smile. Michael smiled back, looking relieved.

"I wish you were my governess," Richard teased as they walked side-by-side along the pier.

"You, sir, *need* a governess. . .to keep you at your books!"

Richard chuckled at the come-back while Sarah sat down beneath the sun-shade she'd brought along.

"I thought you were going to help Libby and Rachel."

"I changed my mind," Sarah said on a tired sigh. "I need a rest."

Richard sat down beside her as Sarah took off her bonnet. She smelled of fresh air and her feet were covered with sand—so was the hem of her skirts, but she didn't seem to care. In fact, she looked comfortable, completely natural, in this environment.

"Is everything going well at the captain's house?" Richard asked. "I mean, with Gretchen. . ."

"Everything is fine, although I try to stay out of Mrs. Schlyterhaus' way."

Richard nodded. "That's probably wise. At least until Gretchen gets used to having you around."

Sarah smiled.

Richard cleared his throat. "My parents asked me to invite you and the children for Sunday dinner after church. Would you come?"

Sarah was a bit surprised by the invitation, although she was glad for it. She had been wondering what to do about church and the children on Sunday.

"Thank you, Richard," she said sincerely. "I'll ask the captain, but I'm sure he won't object. Not if it's an invitation from you and your family. However, I get the impression that the Sinclairs aren't Christians. The captain won't mind me taking his children to church, will he?"

"I don't think so. The children have been to a few Sunday school classes because my mother teaches. She's invited them out every now and then, and the captain has never objected."

"Oh, well, that's good," Sarah said with a smile. "Then, yes, with the captain's permission, I'd love to come on Sunday."

Richard nodded and returned her smile. He thought Sarah was the prettiest young lady he'd ever seen. And, not only was she pretty, but she had a heart for the Lord and a sense of humor that even he, Richard, could appreciate.

Oh, Lord, he silently prayed, *is it possible for a man to fall in love in less than three days? If it is, then I believe I've succumbed!*

Richard had never been interested in any one woman, not seriously, anyway. Then again, no one woman he'd met was like Sarah McCabe.

"Well, I'd best get back to work," he said abruptly, "but I'll see you this evening. . ." Then he just couldn't help teasing her. "Unless, of course, you're too. . .*sunburned!*"

"I will not be sunburned!" Sarah retorted. Then she arranged her skirts so they covered her feet and fixed the sun-shade so it protected her arms and face.

Richard chuckled as he left the beach.

seven

The concert at the Shubert Theatre was delightful. Sarah, being a music teacher, considered herself a tough critic. However, the ensemble played without a flaw. Then, after the concert, they walked over to the ice cream parlor.

Richard's friends were good company—for the most part. Nickolina, or "Lina" as she preferred, was Richard's cousin, and she and Sarah got along well from the beginning, as Lina was a teacher, too, at an elementary school. Sarah then learned that Lina was betrothed to a dashing young man named Timothy Barnes who was in attendance that night as well. Mr. Barnes was an expressman who delivered packages, parcels, and mail. Mr. Barnes' younger brother, Lionel, also came along for the concert, but he was unlike his brother, and Sarah found him to be rather obnoxious.

And then there was Bethany Stafford.

Bethany was a quiet and melancholy young woman of seventeen years. She had gray eyes and what Sarah thought was nondescript brown hair. Sarah soon realized that Bethany had designs on Richard, who was being quite solicitous toward Sarah, and Sarah felt the chill of Bethany's stare more than once. And the chill had nothing to do with ice cream, either. Nor was it quiet and melancholy. It spoke volumes!

"It was nice of you to walk me back to the captain's home, Richard," Sarah said later.

He grinned. "Well, I wasn't about to let Lionel take you."

"Thank you for that." Sarah smiled. Then, as moments passed, she furrowed her brows. "I just hope Bethany won't be upset. . . that you're walking me home, I mean. . ."

Richard seemed to think about it for a moment before he shrugged. However, he didn't say anything else about her, so Sarah didn't ask.

"How's your sunburn?"

Sarah stifled a groan. "It smarts, all right." Her forearms, where she'd rolled up her sleeves, the bridge of her nose, her cheeks, and the back of her neck were pink from the outing today with the children. Sarah had applied a good amount of cold cream on the areas in hopes they wouldn't tan.

Richard chuckled.

"Well, I suppose it was worth it since Gabriel eventually caught a fish. It was really something of a beast, too. You should have seen it! Gabriel was so pleased. I think he wanted to impress his father."

"And? Was the captain impressed?"

Sarah's heart sank as she recalled the disappointment on Gabriel's face. "The captain didn't come home when he said he would, and Isabelle had to fillet and cook the fish before she left. It would have spoiled by tomorrow, since the thing didn't fit into the ice box. So the captain won't get to see the fish—whole, anyway."

"The captain is a hard one to keep on a schedule," Richard said with a note of weariness. "It's miraculous when it happens. However, I will defend him by saying that he does love his children very much."

Sarah smiled. "And who knows better than you, his faithful steward!"

Richard returned the compliment with a smile of his own as they reached the captain's residence. He walked Sarah up to the porch.

"I had a very nice evening, Richard. Thank you."

"It was entirely my pleasure," he said, bowing slightly.

Sarah had to suppress a giggle. Even when he wasn't trying to be funny, he was funny.

"I'll come for you after breakfast on Sunday," he stated on a more serious note. "About eight o'clock. All right?"

Sarah nodded. "Captain Sinclair has given his approval, so the children and I will be waiting."

She let herself into the house, dark now except for a single lamp shining from the hallway. She made a move to extinguish it, but then Gretchen caught her with a shout.

"Leave it on! Captain Sinclair will be home late. I always leave a light on for him. Don't touch it!"

"Yes, ma'am," Sarah replied. Then she made her way upstairs, using the servant's stairwell, glad that she had remembered. She was having trouble in that regard, since she wasn't accustomed to being a "servant."

In her room, she prepared for bed. Then she decided to write to her parents. She told them about the captain and his children. She mentioned Richard and Lina and the concert tonight. She wrote about Gretchen, and asked for prayers. But, later, as she closed her eyes for sleep, Bethany Stafford was who came to mind.

What's her story? Sarah wondered. *And why, like Mrs. Schlyterhaus, did she seem to take an immediate dislike to me?* It made her angry and she wanted to dislike both Bethany and Mrs. Schlyterhaus right back!

But then Sarah recalled a passage of scripture where Jesus said, "Love your enemies, bless them that curse you, do good to them that hate you, and pray for them which despitefully use you, and persecute you. . . ."

Turning over in her soft, fluffy bed, Sarah sighed and whispered. "All right, Lord. I will most certainly try. . ."

❧

The thunder and lightning awoke Sarah early the next morning. She crawled out of bed and padded to the enormous closet. *My! Even this closet is grand!* she thought. Then, donning a warm robe against the damp chill in her bedroom, Sarah took her Bible in hand and began her morning devotions.

Later, after she had washed and dressed, she went down to the kitchen. Isabelle was there, cooking breakfast. They bid each other a good morning as Sarah poured herself a glass of freshly squeezed orange juice. However, she would wait for the captain and the children before eating breakfast.

"This is such a beautiful house," she said, looking around the room. "Even this kitchen is beautiful."

"Sure it is," Isabelle replied with a broad smile. "I'm glad to work here."

"Me, too." After only a few days, Sarah was beginning to think she'd like to stay here the rest of her life.

The children woke up, and Sarah supervised their washing and dressing. The three older ones managed almost completely on their own, but little Rachel needed assistance each step of the way. When at last they came downstairs, the captain was already at the table. He chatted with his children while Isabelle served breakfast. Then Sarah announced that she would begin piano lessons today.

"It seems a good day for it," she added.

"I'll say!" The captain replied as a loud clap of thunder reverberated over the house.

Rachel, sitting up in her junior chair, covered her ears. "I don't yike dat!" she wailed.

"Well, now, thunder can't hurt you, darling," the captain said tenderly. "Don't be afraid."

Sarah's heart fairly skipped a beat. *What would it be like to have Kyle Sinclair call me "darling,"* she couldn't help but wonder. His voice had been so low and soft just now when he'd spoken to little Rachel.

Embarrassed by her thoughts, Sarah immediately concentrated on her breakfast.

"If you learn to play a whole piece on the piano by the end of the summer," the captain promised his children as the conversation returned to their lessons, "and if I can *recognize* the piece," he added with a grin, "then I'll throw a party for you—a recital.

And I'll invite all my friends to come and hear you play."

The children heartily accepted the challenge and seemed quite impressed that their father's friends would come just to hear them play the piano. Even Gabriel looked somewhat enthused.

After breakfast, the captain went about his business while Sarah situated the children in the music room. It was located at the end of the hallway between the ladies' parlor and the men's parlor—not to be confused with the reception parlor. And Sarah was again amazed. *This house has a room for everything!* she decided.

Opening up some sheets of music, which she'd brought with her from the academy in Chicago, Sarah began the piano lessons. However, before the children could actually play, they had to learn to read the notes. Much to Sarah's delight, they learned quickly. By lunch time, Gabriel, Michael, and Libby could play one of the primary tunes.

"Can we have the party now?" Libby asked.

"Not quite yet," Sarah replied. She was sure that the captain expected to hear more than a basic four-note piece.

"Father! Father! Listen to what I can play!" Libby shouted, running down the stairs to meet the captain as he arrived home later that night. She was in her nightgown, and Sarah was embarrassed that she couldn't catch her.

"I'm sorry, Captain."

He waved a hand in the air. "It's all right, Sarah." Scooping Libby into his arms, he carried her toward the music room. "I would be happy to hear what you can play."

As Sarah stood at the doorway, Libby played her little song. When she finished, the captain applauded loudly.

"Such talent!" he exclaimed, with a wink at Sarah. "I'm so proud of you, Libby!"

The little girl was beaming. Then she ran into her father's lap.

"Now, Libby, it's bedtime," Sarah said on a note of admonishment. She wanted the captain to know she was doing her job.

"Sarah, why don't you call down the other children and then you play for us?" Captain Sinclair suggested. "A bedtime melody."

"Oh, yes!" cried Libby.

Somewhat embarrassed, Sarah shrugged. "Well. . .if you'd like me to play, I will."

"I would like you to play."

With a nod, Sarah left the music room and collected the boys. Rachel was already asleep for the night. Then she sat down at the piano and began to play. Her long, slender fingers danced above the ivory keys in practiced motions. A piece from Chopin first. Then Mozart. A Brahms lullaby next. And, finally, one of her favorite hymns: "Be Still, My Soul."

When Sarah finished playing, she sighed. That last piece never failed to stir her heart. In the next moment, however, she remembered her audience. Turning around, her eyes met the captain's.

"That was beautiful, Sarah," he said quietly. His black eyes shone beneath the pale glow of the lamplight.

"Thank you, Captain," she replied demurely. Sarah could barely pull her eyes away from his gaze.

Then suddenly the captain grinned. "But now look what you've done."

Sarah smiled, noticing all of the children had fallen fast asleep.

Standing with a sleeping Libby in his arms, the captain said, "I'll carry her, if you'll wake the boys. They're old enough to stumble up to bed."

She nodded, gently shaking Michael first, then Gabriel. They moaned and groaned and stomped up the front staircase, angry to have been awakened.

With the task completed, and the children all in their beds now, Sarah met the captain in the hallway.

"I've made a decision tonight," he announced.

"A decision, Captain? And what might that be?" Sarah wondered if a new rule was about to be instated. Something, perhaps, about the children being down in the music room, dressed in their bed clothes well after their bedtime. . .

"I've decided," the captain said softly, "that I'm going to do whatever it takes to keep you here, Sarah McCabe. You're good for my children, I can see that already. And, tonight, for the first time ever, I felt like a family-man instead of a businessman. I have you to thank for that."

Sarah was so stunned, she didn't know what to say.

But the captain didn't seem to expect a reply. He merely smiled and bade her a good night. Then he turned and went downstairs.

Alone in the large hallway, Sarah experienced a tumult of emotions. She would love to live in this house forever, and she couldn't help but wonder at the look in the captain's eyes when he said he had decided to "keep her here." Could that have been a romantic gleam shining from their dark depths?

Hardly! she thought. *I'm imagining things! Didn't Leah always tell me I have a runaway imagination?* Sarah sighed heavily. *I should have never read the Bronte sisters' books!*

However, to serve as something of a reality check, Sarah mentioned the incident to Richard the following day after the worship service. She felt she could trust Richard. He was practical and they were friends.

Richard smiled. "He said that? That he's going to do 'whatever it takes'?"

Sarah nodded, looking down at Rachel in her lap. Gabriel, Michael, and Libby were in the back of the wagon as they rode to the Navis' home. "What do you think about it, Richard?" she ventured.

He grinned rather sheepishly. "I think maybe I'll help him. . . keep you here, that is."

He chuckled when Sarah lifted her eyes heavenward, shaking her head.

"I should have known better than to ask you a serious question!" she charged.

Richard only chuckled again. "Aw, Sarah, I'm just kidding." Then he put on his best, most serious expression. "Captain Sinclair has hired many governesses in the last few years. Personally, I think Gretchen scares them away."

Could be the snakes, Sarah thought, remembering what Gabriel and Michael had confessed.

"Anyway," Richard continued, "I suppose the captain has seen how well you manage the children. . .and Gretchen. . .and he doesn't want to lose you. That only seems logical."

Turning to Sarah, he raised his brows as if waiting for her to agree.

She did. And of course she had imagined that look in the captain's eyes last night; it wasn't a romantic gleam at all, but a look of. . .of desperation! The poor man. He couldn't afford to lose another governess!

Richard continued to drive the wagon west on Lisbon Plank toll road.

"How much farther?" Sarah asked.

"Less than a mile."

Farm fields now stretched out as far as the eye could see. They had left the city behind, though they were still in Milwaukee, Richard informed her. Out here, near Western Avenue (or North 35th Street), it was all rural area. Moreover, the temperature was a good ten degrees warmer than it had been closer to Lake Michigan.

"Once you cross the river," Richard explained, "it's hotter. And, in the winter, it's colder. However, nearer to the lake, you never can escape the humidity."

Sarah nodded. "St. Louis is that way, too. Except, we have both during the summer months—the heat and humidity. It's ghastly!"

Richard grinned. Then, minutes later, he turned the wagon onto a neat gravel driveway which split in half to form a large circle that passed in front of his house. At the porch, he let them off.

Sarah took his hand as she alighted from the wagon, noticing that this part of the driveway was all brick, like the house. Then, in two sweeping glances, she surveyed the grounds. To her right was an apple orchard next to a small pond. To her left was another orchard, but it stood behind rows of flowers.

"What a lovely place," she murmured.

Richard smiled at her comment. "The house is quite unique. However, we're just average folks and this is a typical farm."

"But it doesn't seem 'typical.' And this house looks like a country mansion! Why, it's much larger than any farm house I've ever seen!"

Richard smiled and nodded, looking pleased. "My father inherited a good sum of money and used it to build this house. His 'dream house' you might call it. He patterned it after his aunt's villa in Germany, where he had spent some time as a child. He loved it there, so when she left my father money, he decided to honor her in this way. With this." With one hand, he made a great sweeping gesture toward the house. "My father finished building it in 1851."

"How fascinating!" Sarah exclaimed. She had never been to another country before, and she was in awe of anyone who had.

"The farm part of our property is out back," Richard continued. "We've got hogs, cows, sheep, chickens, a vegetable garden, a corn field, a wheat field, and a grove of pear trees."

"I see," she replied politely, though Sarah wasn't interested in that. She'd grown up around farms and fields. What appealed to her now was the genteel city life.

Richard's parents' wagon pulled into the circle drive. Sarah gathered the captain's children while Richard helped his father down from the wagon and into his wheel chair. Sarah had already met Mr. and Mrs. Navis at church, and the children were well acquainted with them from previous visits. Mrs. Navis asked Sarah inside while Richard and his father took the children out back to the barn to see the kittens.

"The Staffords should be arriving soon," said Mrs. Navis.

"Richard told us you met Bethany Stafford on Friday evening."

"Yes, I did," Sarah replied, and she had been praying for Bethany ever since.

Mrs. Navis took off her bonnet and then showed Sarah around the house. The furnishings weren't elegant at all, like they were in the captain's home. Here, the furniture was large and sturdy and everywhere handmade quilts and knitted blankets covered faded upholstery. Sarah was reminded of her parents' home in Missouri.

"Can I help you prepare dinner?" Sarah asked Mrs. Navis as they entered the large kitchen.

"Sure can. I'm roasting a couple of chickens."

In this heat? Sarah thought.

"Then I'll bake up some biscuits and set out some of the pickles I canned last year. How does that sound?"

"Sounds hot," Sarah replied in all honesty. "Except for the pickles."

Bea only laughed and waved her into the cellar. "I've got a summer kitchen down here."

Sarah glanced around at the white-washed walls, cupboards, and large wood-burning stove and oven. It was nearly fifteen degrees cooler down here. Then Bea led her into the fruit cellar where numerous glass jars stood on paper-lined shelves.

"We'll have some applesauce, too," she declared, grabbing a few jars.

Minutes later, Richard brought in two freshly killed chickens. "I had the boys help me pluck and clean them," he told Sarah and his mother.

"A good job for those boys," Bea replied.

"And we all put on aprons," he added for Sarah's benefit. "They haven't ruined their good clothes. . .but give them time."

Sarah smiled. "Where are Libby and Rachel?"

"They're with Pops on the back porch, holding the kittens."

"Pops?" Sarah giggled for the name sounded funny to her. "You don't really call your father *Pops*, do you?"

"Sure, I do," Richard replied while his mother nodded, feigning a helpless expression. "He's Pops and she's. . .Mops. Mops and Pops."

He chuckled at his attempt at humor, while Mrs. Navis raised an annoyed brow. "Mops, you say?"

Sarah shook her head. "You poor, poor woman," she teased, "having to put up with his bad jokes."

He brought his chin back, as if insulted. "That wasn't a bad joke, Sarah."

"The worst I've heard," she retorted.

Bea laughed with shoulders shaking. Richard was now the one wearing the annoyed expression.

"An ally!" Bea declared, putting an arm around Sarah. "At last I have an ally!"

eight

Shortly after Mrs. Navis got the chickens into the oven, the Staffords arrived with their eight children. Bethany, who was the oldest of them, looked surprised to see Sarah. Then she chose to ignore Sarah's existence altogether. Minutes later, Richard's Aunt Ruth and Uncle Jesse showed up. Lina was with them, along with her fiance Tim.

"Oh, Sarah, it's good to see you again," Lina said, giving her a quick hug that made up for Bethany's lack of friendliness.

After dinner had been prepared, they ate out on the lawn with their plates in their laps. It reminded Sarah of the annual church picnic in Missouri; they ate with plates in their laps then, too.

When they'd finished, Richard helped Sarah carry dishes into the kitchen. "I promised all the children cow rides," he said with a grin.

"Cow rides?"

Richard nodded. "Last time the captain's children were here, I gave them a ride on Lyla's back. She's one of our Guernsey cows, and the children had so much fun that they have requested to do it again."

Sarah smiled. "How fast does Lyla go?"

"About as fast as I can pull her."

They shared a laugh walking back outside. Sarah watched from the back porch as first Libby, then Rachel took a ride on poor Lyla. When their turns came, Gabriel and Michael bounced and shouted, "Giddyup!" However, the cow wasn't very cooperative.

From her place near the kitchen door, Sarah could hear the rattling of pans and dishes. She called to Richard, telling him she was going to help clean up inside. He nodded.

Entering the house, Sarah was surprised to find only Bethany in the kitchen. She was washing the dinner dishes from a large basin of water on a counter with wooden cupboards underneath it.

"Here, let me help you," Sarah said, grabbing a dish towel.

Bethany didn't reply, but Sarah began drying dishes anyway. After a few minutes of uncomfortable silence, Sarah decided to clear the air once and for all.

"Bethany," she began carefully, "have I said or done something to offend you?"

Bethany paused in her washing. "No," she replied at last.

Sarah sighed a dramatic breath of relief. "Well, good. However, I'm under the impression that you dislike me, and I believe it's because of my friendship with Richard. Is that right?"

Bethany stopped washing the plate in her hands. "Your *friendship* with Richard?" She smiled cynically. "Is that what you call it? *A friendship?*"

Setting down the towel, Sarah put her hands on her hips and lifted a defiant chin. "Yes. *Friendship* is most exactly the word I would use! Richard has been very good to me since I arrived in Milwaukee. We both work for Captain Sinclair, and I believe Richard and I are what Charles Dickens referred to in his novel *Great Expectations*. . ." Sarah cleared her throat. "We are 'fellow sufferers.'"

"Oh, hardly!" Bethany retorted.

"Well, we are, too!" Sarah replied, even though she was joking. She very much appreciated her job, but she couldn't help teasing Bethany. "The captain is a very forgetful man, you know, and that places a great burden on Richard and me."

"Yes, I'm sure it does," Bethany said tartly.

"Well, anyway," Sarah continued, "I think Richard has just been kind to me because he wants me to feel comfortable here and make some friends. That's all."

Bethany laughed. "Richard is not that gallant," she stated,

somewhat sarcastically. "Captain Sinclair has had dozens of governesses and Richard never took one of them to the theater or home to meet his family."

Sarah paused to think about this. Perhaps Richard was, indeed, interested in her romantically, though she hadn't thought so until now that Bethany suggested it. Sarah had merely assumed that Richard's attentions were due to politeness and loyalty to the captain—and, maybe, even pity toward her as a new governess in a strange city.

And how do I feel about that? Sarah wondered. In truth, she didn't know. Richard was considerate and witty, and Sarah enjoyed his company; however, he didn't make her heart pound or her knees weak. . .and that was the sort of love Sarah was waiting for. Heart-pounding, knee-weakening love! Like the kind in Longfellow's *Evangeline* or one of Sir Walter Scott's books.

Oh, well, I'll think about love and Richard later, Sarah decided, realizing that there was still this matter of Bethany Stafford to contend with for the moment.

Then suddenly, an idea struck. . .

"Bethany, are you and Richard betrothed?"

The other girl's head shot up with surprise at such a blatant question. Finally she answered, "No."

"Has he spoken to you of marriage?"

Bethany considered Sarah and then shook her head. "No."

"Well, then," Sarah said practically, "he's fair game, so to speak . . .not that I'm interested, of course. I'm merely trying to make a point."

"Who's fair game?"

Sarah's eyes widened at the sound of Richard's voice, coming suddenly from right behind her. She looked over at Bethany who was blushing profusely. *Not much help there!* she decided.

"The chickens!" Sarah finally managed, donning an innocent grin and turning to face Richard. "Wouldn't you agree? The chickens are fair game."

"Oh, yes," Bethany blurted from over the basin of water. "Chickens. Fair game."

Through a narrowed, speculative gaze, Richard looked from Sarah to Bethany and then back to Sarah. He nodded slowly. Then he grinned. "Sure. That's what I thought. The chickens."

Sarah lowered her chin in an effort to conceal a smirk, and beside her, she noticed Bethany doing the same. Richard must have noticed for he mumbled something about Sarah being an instigator as he left the kitchen. She let the comment go since she knew full well that she could get even with Richard later. Then, picking up the next plate from the wooden rack beside the basin, Sarah resumed her job of drying.

Once the dishes were washed and put away, Sarah and Bethany joined everyone else in the yard. Cool evening breezes began to blow, rustling the branches of the apple trees overhead. Gabriel and Michael were at the pond, trying to catch a frog or two, and the little girls were playing hide and seek in the orchard. Bethany was no longer ignoring Sarah. In fact, she was rather friendly since their conversation in the kitchen. She pointed out their neighboring farm and talked of the concert they had heard two nights ago.

Something must have happened in the kitchen, Sarah realized. *I must have somehow won Bethany. . .*

Mrs. Navis discovered the kitchen had been cleaned when she went inside to make coffee. And when she discovered that Sarah and Bethany had cleaned it, she chided them, saying, "No guests of mine clean up the kitchen!"

"But we wanted to help," Sarah told her.

"Nonsense! Now you'll both have to come back next week so I can be a proper hostess!"

"Yes, ma'am," Bethany replied with a tiny smile that almost reached her sad gray eyes. Then, after Mrs. Navis walked away, she leaned over and whispered to Sarah, "She says that every Sunday because every Sunday I clean up for her."

Sarah smiled. "So, why do you do it, Beth?"

She shrugged. "I guess I just feel that Mrs. Navis has so much to do since Mr. Navis was maimed in the war."

Sarah nodded her understanding and sensed Bethany had a real heart for this family.

But where is Richard's heart? she couldn't help but wonder. She supposed it wasn't any of her business. What Richard said or did shouldn't concern her one bit. After all, she revelled in her freedom of being unwed. She had her independence, and Richard could have Bethany!

"My aunt and uncle have offered to take you home," Richard said later, as the sun began to set. He was standing on the lawn, near the front porch, and Sarah thought he looked quite handsome with the orange sky in the background.

And I shouldn't even care! she told herself.

"Are you listening to me?" Richard said with a grin.

"Yes, of course I am," Sarah blurted, sounding defensive to her own ears.

"I said my aunt and uncle—"

"I heard that." Sarah lowered her lashes, softening her tone of voice. "And that's very kind of them."

"Well, they don't live far from the captain, so it's no trouble." He chuckled and nodded to where the children were playing. "The 'trouble' will be rounding up those children."

Sarah had to agree.

And it took a while, but finally the children were gathered up and loaded into the large buggy.

"I'll see you tomorrow," Richard said.

Sarah nodded and couldn't help but notice the light of promise in his blue eyes.

Then, riding back to the captain's residence, she wondered whether Richard was truly interested in her romantically, as Bethany presumed, or if this, like her thoughts of Captain Sinclair, were mere imaginings.

❧

Wednesday was Sarah's first day off and, after Aurora Reil came and collected the captain's children, she sat down and made note of all she had to do today. She had, among other tasks, her laundry to do, and Gretchen was a help in telling her of a woman whose fees were reasonable. She explained to Sarah that when a working woman has but one day off, it should not be spent doing laundry.

"You'll be no good to anyone," Gretchen said sternly, "if you don't have something of a rest."

Sarah smiled, glad that Mrs. Schlyterhaus wasn't berating her as usual.

"Even God took a rest," the woman added in a thick German accent, "after He made the vorld."

Sarah's smile broadened. "Are you a Christian, Mrs. Schlyterhaus?"

At the question, Gretchen frowned heavily. "It is none of your business what I am or vhat I am not!"

Sarah gasped. "Oh, but I didn't mean. . .what I meant was. . ."

The older woman scowled. "Irish!" she fairly spat at Sarah before walking away.

Stunned, Sarah could only wonder at that last comment.

Later, she asked Richard when he "happened" to stop by. "What did Mrs. Schlyterhaus mean by calling me 'Irish'? That is to say, I am of Irish decent, but—"

"It's not you, personally, Sarah. It's just that. . .well, it seems Gretchen isn't a very forgiving person and your being Irish just gives her an excuse not to be friendly. I believe Gretchen knows the Lord, but she refuses to exercise forgiveness toward others."

As they sat together on the front porch, Richard continued to explain. "About ten or fifteen years ago, the Germans and the Irish were at war with each other here in Milwaukee. Each had claimed its own section of the city and, if one wandered into the other's area, there was a bloody fight—or sometimes a riot. Gretchen's husband was killed in one of those riots."

"How awful!" Sarah exclaimed.

Richard nodded. "Later, when a law was proposed to ban alcohol here in Milwaukee, the Germans and the Irish—both known to like their beer—joined forces and rallied, or perhaps I should say *rioted*, against the proposed law."

"They must have won, too," Sarah murmured, "for I've noticed that there's a tavern on practically every corner of this city!"

Richard chuckled. "That there is, my dear Sarah McCabe. However, sometimes I wonder if Gretchen still believes she's at war with the Irish." He smiled. "But please don't be too concerned about it. You're perfectly safe. I'll make sure of it."

Then Richard searched her face in a way that gave Sarah yet another indication he might be interested in her. She felt herself blush and quickly lowered her gaze.

"Will you allow me to take you to dinner tonight?" he asked.

Sarah looked up to find a very solemn expression on his face. Then he glanced at his pocket watch. "I have some time. . .before I need to be home. . ."

Curious, Sarah asked, "Do you have an appointment tonight, Richard?"

He smiled and shook his head. "No. Only chores."

"Chores? You mean that after working all day for the captain, you go home and do farm chores?"

Richard nodded. "My father can't manage many of them anymore, so I do most of the work. We have, however, hired planters this year."

"But still. . .you must be exhausted!"

He grinned. "Not too exhausted to take you to dinner. Will you come?"

Sarah thought about it, wondering if she should encourage Richard this way. She didn't want to give him false hopes, and yet she liked his company. He made her lonesome for her brothers.

"What do you say, Sarah?"

"Well, I don't know. . ."

"We can ask Lina and Tim to join us if that will make you feel more comfortable."

"That's not necessary."

Richard lifted a teasing brow. "You're not afraid of me?"

Sarah swallowed a giggle. "Not in the least!"

Richard shrugged, indicating that perhaps she ought to be, and this time Sarah laughed aloud. Oh, how he could make her laugh with a mere facial expression or a simple shrug of his broad shoulders.

"Will you dine with me or not?" he asked in mock irritation. "I'm hungry."

"Ten minutes to freshen up?" she pleaded, donning one of her sweetest smiles.

Richard glanced at his watch again. "Ten minutes."

Sarah scurried into the house. She only took five minutes to splash water onto her face and check the pins in her hair. Leaving her bedroom, she grabbed a light wrapper, just in case the wind shifted abruptly as it was known to do here in Milwaukee.

"Ready?" Richard asked, meeting her in the foyer under Gretchen's scowling countenance.

"Ready." Sarah chanced a look at the housekeeper. "Good night, Mrs. Schlyterhaus."

"I lock the doors at eight o'clock on Vednesdays," she stated firmly. "If you're not home by then, I vill lock you out!"

When Sarah gasped, Richard gave her elbow a squeeze and whispered, "I have a key. Don't worry." He smiled at Gretchen then and wished her a good night.

Laughing softly at Richard's cleverness, the two left Captain Sinclair's residence for a river-side cafe.

What Sarah learned about Richard that night amazed her. First of all, he knew almost everyone at the restaurant. Several businessmen greeted him by name.

"Did you take me here to impress me?" Sarah asked impishly when the proprietor seated them at one of his best tables.

"Sure I did," Richard replied with a grin.

Secondly, he was honest. And he was a hard worker—Sarah saw the telltale signs worn into his hands. They were the hands of a working man. A farmer. And yet, there was an air of sophistication about him, a manner that came from education.

However, what impressed Sarah the most was Richard's

generosity. Not only with his money, for the meal was surely a costly one, but Richard gave of himself. Like the way he helped his father and the captain; the way he managed Mrs. Schlyterhaus by not getting in her way, but around her instead. He seemed to strive to appease and accommodate, but never to the extent of compromising his faith.

My father would like him, Sarah found herself thinking. So would my brothers—especially Luke, that rascal!

"What are you thinking about?" Richard suddenly asked. "You're smiling."

Sarah's smile broadened. "I was thinking of my brother Luke. You remind me of him."

Richard lifted a brow. "If I remember correctly, that's not always good."

"It's only *not* good when I'm in trouble," Sarah replied, causing Richard to chuckle heartily.

After supper, they decided against the hackney and walked back to the captain's home. The evening temperature was mild, even with the Lake Michigan breezes, so their stroll together was enjoyable.

"I'll have to take you roller skating some time," Richard remarked. "It's quite the rage in Milwaukee right now. We have several brand new rinks, in fact."

"Really?" Sarah had heard of roller skates. The wooden-wheeled toys had been invented in New York several years ago. "Well, that would be fun, Richard," she said at last.

Finally they reached the captain's house. On the side porch, Richard turned the knob. The door opened.

"Not quite eight o'clock," he said, looking sheepish.

Then suddenly, he became serious. He leaned forward and placed a gentle kiss on Sarah's cheek. His expression, as he told her good night, made Sarah realize that he meant business. The courtship sort of business. The whole business Sarah tried to avoid. Why couldn't they just be friends?

Oh, dear Lord, she prayed, forgetting herself and climbing the front stairwell. *Now what do I do?*

nine

"Captain, may I enroll the children in swimming lessons?"

Captain Sinclair lifted his dark gaze from the papers on his desk. "Swimming lessons?" He frowned slightly. "They already know how to swim."

"Yes, I know. I've seen them at the lake. However, the boys are so energetic. . ."

The captain laughed. "You're seeking to take the, uh, wind out of their sails, are you?"

Sarah smiled. "Yes, exactly."

He laughed once more.

"The swimming lessons would be perfect. They begin at eight o'clock every weekday morning and go until noon. The swimming school, as it's called, is right on the river."

"Yes. I know the one. It's north of here."

"That's it, Captain."

He nodded. "All right. You may enroll the children, Sarah."

"Thank you, sir."

Sarah left the captain's office, thinking it would be a perfect solution. It would solve the problem of the boys' exuberance and get her away from the house during the time Richard usually stopped by every day, usually mid-morning. She had decided to put some distance between them. Hopefully out-of-sight would mean out-of-mind. For both of them!

However, such was not the case. Richard soon began visiting her at the swimming school since he couldn't catch her at the captain's home. Then he always drove Sarah and the children back in the Owensboro wagon or sleek black buggy—whichever of the captain's vehicles he had that day. And he obtained the captain's permission to make these visits, which impressed Sarah. Captain

Sinclair obviously valued Richard greatly to grant him such allowances.

Sarah, too, couldn't help but grow fonder of him each day. Richard was quick-witted and he made her laugh. The children adored him and he added more fun to their days. Like stopping for ice cream or candy sticks. Or telling Bible stories in the most interesting, most amusing way as they picnicked on the front lawn of the prestigious Sinclair home—in spite of Gretchen's disapproving frowns at their "cluttering up the captain's yard."

Finally Sarah gave up. There was no point in trying to avoid Richard; he was unavoidable. Besides, when he wasn't around, because the captain's business kept him away, Sarah actually found herself missing his company!

Then one Sunday, when he came to get them for the worship service, Sarah noticed a change in him. There was suddenly a seriousness about him, and it caused Sarah to grow concerned. All too soon, however, she learned what he was up to.

"Sarah, I know you said you enjoy your independence," Richard began. "I know you said that you've chosen to be unmarried. But I was thinking. . ."

"Don't, Richard!" Sarah said on a note of warning. She sensed what was coming and she didn't want to hurt him.

"But it's not proper for us to be such good friends. . .without some sort of commitment."

Sarah lowered her gaze to her gloved hands, folded in her lap. "Yes. I suppose you're right."

They rode for a few minutes in silence, both busy with their thoughts. Then, after they'd arrived at the church, Richard spoke again.

"Will you think about it, Sarah? About allowing me to court you? I'll write to your father and ask his permission." With that he helped her down from the wagon.

"I'll think about it," Sarah replied quickly. Then she gathered the captain's brood and marched them into the church.

Later that day, however, after they'd eaten supper, Richard managed to persuade Sarah into taking a walk around the farm.

Again the discussion of courtship came up.

"I like you very much, Richard," Sarah told him. "In fact, I was looking forward to your company today. . .at least until—"

"Until I had to ruin everything just before the worship service."

Sarah had to suppress a giggle in spite of the seriousness of the moment. "Yes. That's right. You ruined everything," she replied teasingly.

Richard smiled. "Well, it couldn't be helped. As I said, I've been thinking."

"Richard, you don't know what you're getting into," Sarah stated earnestly. "We've known each other just a short time. . .and you don't know my family. My brothers. I always felt sorry for my suitors; my brothers gave them such a terrible time. And then my father, being a pastor, drilled them mercilessly." She shook her head. "It's a wonder my sister Leah managed to get married. My brothers did that to her, too, although not to the same extent."

Richard was smiling nevertheless. "Something tells me I'll be able to handle your brothers, Sarah."

She smiled right back. "You probably will. . ."

Raising his brows, Richard asked, "Does that mean yes?"

"No!" she replied impishly.

He laughed as they walked near the cornfield.

"Richard," Sarah said seriously, taking his arm and pulling him to a halt, "I don't know how to say this except to just come out and say it." She sighed. "Richard, I don't think I love you. . .I don't know if I ever will."

Much to her surprise, he didn't seem hurt. He merely smiled and said, "What do you think a courtship is for? It gives a couple permission to get to know each other. . .to fall in love."

Sarah sighed once more and shook her head. "I don't know. When my father hears of your interest in me—and that I *allowed* you to write to him—he'll tell my mother, who will immediately begin wedding preparations. She'll tell my brothers, of course, which will bring Luke home and then you'll be sorry, Richard, because if Luke comes home, he'll be expecting a wedding. And there are all my cousins. When they find out, particularly my cousin Brian, who resembles Luke in thought, word, and mischievous deed, they'll—"

Richard quieted Sarah's ramblings by touching a finger to her lips. "Perhaps we should worry about all that at the precise moment it arises."

Sarah rolled her eyes heavenward. "You sound like my brother Benjamin. He can be so very practical."

Richard grinned. "Thank you." Then he pulled a folded piece of paper from his shirt pocket and handed it to Sarah. "This is the letter I wrote to your father. I'd like you to read it and, if you agree and accept its terms, I'll post it tomorrow. Will you do that? Will you read it and think over everything I've said?"

"Yes," Sarah replied taking the letter. "I'll do that."

They turned and, as they headed for the house again, Sarah spotted Bethany sitting on the front porch. She could see Bethany watching them intently. If Sarah had won her friendship last week, she had surely lost it this week.

"Perhaps you should talk with her," Sarah suggested, nodding her head toward Bethany. "I think she's going to be hurt if you start courting me."

"I wish Bethany's father wouldn't have put ideas into her head in the first place." At Sarah's questioning gaze, he explained. "Paul Stafford owns the neighboring farm and long ago, when Bethany and I were still children, he got this notion that it would be great to combine the properties via a marriage between Bethany and me." Richard looked into Sarah's deep blue eyes. "Only problem with that idea is. . .I don't love Bethany."

His eyes locked with hers in what Richard hoped was a meaningful gaze. Sarah didn't turn away, as if meeting his challenge.

"So you'll talk to her then?" she asked softly.

Richard nodded. "I'll talk to her. . .although I don't relish having to do it."

ಜ

But later that evening, after Sarah and the children had left with Lina and Tim, Richard asked Bethany if he could walk her home.

"I need to speak with you," he said. They took the long, winding path that went around the vegetable garden. "It's about Sarah. I've written to her father and asked permission to court her. I thought you should know."

Bethany said nothing for several steps.

"I've prayed about this," Richard added. "I think Sarah is the one He has chosen for me."

Bethany stopped short. "She's going to break your heart! She's a. . .a flirt!"

"No, she's not," Richard stated calmly.

Bethany stood with arms akimbo. "Well, she's certainly very comfortable talking to men. Even my brother Billy noticed. . .and he's only fifteen!"

"Sarah is comfortable talking to men because she has three older brothers, and she's the youngest in the family." Taking a hold of Bethany's elbow, Richard urged her to continue their walk. "You know," he said gently, "sometimes I think younger children have an advantage in that they get to see how things work by observing their siblings. Whereas you and I usually have to experience life by trial and error."

"You're making a mistake, Richard," Bethany maintained in spite of what he'd just said. "Sarah doesn't love you. . ."

"It may not be love yet. But there is something between us." *And it was there from the beginning,* Richard added silently.

"You're making a mistake," Bethany repeated. "She doesn't . . .she can't. . .love you. . .like I do."

Richard was pensive for several long moments. Then, as they reached the back door of the Staffords' home, he said, "I'm sorry, Beth. I really am. But it's not meant to be for us. I'm sure about that much. And I love you, too—but as a sister in Christ."

"That could be enough—enough to start," Bethany replied with tears rimming her eyes.

"That would *never* be enough. And someday you'll thank me for my honesty. Someday when the right man comes along. . ."

But Bethany wouldn't hear anymore. With tears spilling down her cheeks, she ran into the house. The tightly sprung door slammed behind her, and Richard had never felt so awful in his life. He hated to hurt her.

"Please, Lord," he prayed on the way back home, "please give Bethany a sense of understanding. Please free her from these unrealistic thoughts of marriage to me. As the Bible says, 'The truth shall make you free.' Lord, I *had* to tell her the truth."

ﻪ‌ﻋ

Up in her bedroom, once her duties were completed for the day, Sarah unfolded the letter Richard had written to her father. The first page was mostly introduction and some background information about Richard and his family—things he had already told her. Not until Sarah got to the middle of the second page was her full attention captured.

> *While I've only known Sarah a short time,*
> Richard wrote, *I believe I love her.*

Love? Sarah was shocked. She, of course, understood that Richard was interested in her. But love?
She read on. . .

> *This love is not based upon physical attractiveness, although Sarah is a beautiful young lady.*

Beautiful? Shaking her head in wonder, Sarah continued.

> *This love is based upon the Light I see shining from within her. Her concern for others, namely Captain Sinclair's children, is remarkable. Her ability to play the piano and sing are gifts from God, to be sure! Just last Tuesday I heard her singing an old Sunday school hymn to the children and it moved my soul. . .*

Sarah gasped, feeling somewhat embarrassed. She had no idea that Richard heard her playing last Tuesday! He should have made his presence known, the rascal!

Forcing her attention back to the letter once more, Sarah finished reading the remainder of its contents. Then she folded it up. *He loves me,* she thought. After only three and a half weeks, *he loves me. And he's terribly romantic. He thinks I'm beautiful—and not just on the outside, but on the inside, too!*

Sarah wasn't sure if she'd ever had a man love her before, other than family members. No one, that she knew of, had ever considered her "beautiful," although her brothers called her "pretty." That is, pretty silly, pretty sassy, and pretty much a pain in their necks!

Sarah smiled at the memory, and then moved to her bedroom window. Pensively, she brushed the lovely ivory-laced curtain aside and gazed out into the blackness of the back yard. She'd had plenty of suitors who asked to court her. But they had seemed rather insignificant, so her father refused them because of Sarah's lack of interest. She had been taught that courtship was the first step toward marriage. She hadn't wanted to marry any of her past suitors. But did she want to marry Richard?

No. Not now, her heart seemed to reply. *But, perhaps, in the future. . .*

With a heavy sigh, Sarah flounced on her bed. The thick crazy quilt, made of silk, satin, and brocade swatches, enveloped her like a soft hug. She thought about Richard for a good long time. Round and round she went. Did she? Didn't she? Should she? Shouldn't she? Would she? Wouldn't she? And out of all her thoughts and questions, one thing was sure: Next to her brothers, Richard was probably the best friend she would ever know.

Then, suddenly, Sarah knew what she must do.

❧

The next morning before leaving with the children for their swimming lessons, Sarah left a note for Richard. She put it in an envelope along with the letter he'd written to her father. The note for Richard was two words long. It said, "Post it."

Richard read Sarah's note and couldn't believe his eyes. *Post it! Post the letter to her father! Glory hallelujah!*

He had prayed himself to sleep last night, asking for God's will in this situation and for help to accept that plan for his life, whether it be with Sarah, or without her. However, this was exactly what he'd hoped; he had been given his heart's desire!

Going about his business routine that day, Richard did every chore with renewed enthusiasm. Some of his coworkers noticed and teasingly asked if he were trying to minimize their efforts by working twice as hard.

"Just feel especially good today," Richard replied with a grin.

One of the customers chuckled. "Seems a mite late for spring fever, hey boy? It's nearly July!"

"This isn't spring fever," Richard retorted, wearing a secret little smile. "Can't you see I'm in love?"

Everyone in the shop hooted. Richard Navis in love? Never!

"There ain't a woman alive who'd have you," teased another coworker.

"Well, I didn't say she loved me back," Richard replied good-naturedly.

They laughed again and had more fun doing their jobs that afternoon since Otis Lazinski spilled a barrel of crude oil and they all skied off the loading dock while trying to help him clean it up!

That evening, as he saddled his horse and then headed for home, Richard allowed his imagination to wander. He had ideas. Big ideas. He'd been thinking about quitting his job with the captain at the end of August and then buying his father's farm.

Pops will be pleased, he thought. *After all, that's what he's wanted all along—his only son to carry on the family farm. To work the land as he did before the war disabled him.*

And Richard loved his animals and the field work. He loved being outside amidst all that God had created. True, the hours of back-breaking labor were gruesome; however, the fruits of that labor were awfully sweet! To take a seed, plant it, and watch it grow into something life sustaining was utterly rewarding for Richard. Much more rewarding than the captain's book work, that's for sure!

And Mama. . .Mama will faint with happiness, Richard decided with a smile. *Sarah will fill that farmhouse with her music and her laughter and, God willing, there will be children. Lots of children. Mama always wanted lots of grandchildren. . .*

Richard smiled. He had big ideas, all right. Now all he had to do was win Sarah's heart!

ten

"This is the most beautiful room I've ever seen!" Sarah exclaimed, glancing at the sculptured plaster work on the ceiling, the two crystal chandeliers which hung from it, and finally the matching crystal wall sconces. This was the first time Sarah had been up on the third floor of this house, inside the formal ballroom.

Captain Sinclair turned from the windows. "Do you like it, Sarah?"

"I should say I do!"

He chuckled softly and his deep voice echoed through the room. The hardwood parquet floor gleamed beneath its new coat of wax, and the tables lining the walls were covered with freshly washed and starched linen cloths.

"I see Gretchen has already begun to prepare for the party on Friday night," the captain observed. Then he turned to Sarah. "I'd like the children dressed formally so they can make an appearance." He grinned. "I enjoy showing off my children."

"Yes, Captain," Sarah replied with a smile.

"And you, too."

Sarah raised questioning brows and the captain laughed.

"Plan on making an appearance," he said between chuckles. "I didn't mean to imply that I'd enjoy showing you off, although—" The captain raised a dark brow as he considered Sarah in two sweeping glances. "I may enjoy it at that."

Sarah flushed, but she chose to laugh off the remark and treat it as though the captain were teasing her. However, when he said things like that or scrutinized her with those black eyes, Sarah felt weak-kneed and nervous.

Uncomfortable, she continued to look around the ballroom.

There was a stage at one end prepared for musicians. And a piano. . .

Goodness! she thought. *Imagine two pianos in one household!*

Sarah turned back to the captain. "Is Richard coming on Friday night?"

"Yes. He'll be here in case I need him to explain my books." Captain Sinclair rubbed his palms together. "Hopefully Friday night we will secure several new shipping deals." He glanced at Sarah. "Elise Kingsley will be here—her late husband owned Great Lakes Shipping. The poor woman has no idea how to run the business, so I've been trying to help her out." He grinned sardonically. "Actually, I want her business for myself—at any price. But that's why I have Richard. And Friday night," he said, waving his hand in two quick sweeps, "this room will be filled with Milwaukee's biggest beer barons."

"Beer barons, sir?"

Captain Sinclair nodded. "Frederick Miller; Jacob Best's son, Phillip; Captain Fred Pabst; and Valentine Blatz, to name a few. It ought to be very interesting."

"And all those men make beer?" Sarah asked.

"They do," the captain replied. "And they're rich, Sarah. Very, very rich." He smiled indulgently. "Have you ever tasted beer, Sarah?"

She shook her head. Her father preached against partaking of strong drink such as beer.

"Well, perhaps you can have a small glass on Friday night after the children are asleep. Just to taste it."

Sarah shook her head, trying to think of how she could politely refuse.

"Do you know how to waltz?" the captain asked her now.

"I know the basics." Sarah's mother had wanted all the McCabe children to know how to dance as part of their education. However, Sarah had never actually done it except with Leah as her partner.

"Come here," the captain said, holding his arms out to her.

Sarah froze, hearing her mother's voice warning her never to dance with a man unless she was sure of his intentions. *It's best to wait until you're betrothed,* her mother had said. *Dancing is a very intimate thing. . .*

"Captain Sinclair, I—"

"Oh, come here," he said with an amused grin. "I'm not going to bite you."

Sarah forced a smile. "Well, yes, I know, but—"

The captain chuckled and came forward in two great strides. "Here," he said, putting an arm around Sarah's waist. Then he took her right hand in his left. He smiled down into her face. "Let's waltz."

Against her better judgment, Sarah didn't protest. *This won't last long,* she told herself. *Leah always said I was a terrible dancer; I stepped on her toes constantly.* Feeling awkward, Sarah looked down.

"Ah-ah-ah," the captain said on a note of admonition. "Don't look at your feet. Look at me. Your partner. And follow my lead."

Sarah tried to relax in the captain's embrace and she nearly lost herself in his deep dark eyes as they slowly waltzed down one length of the ballroom.

"Very good," he said with a smile. "Now pick up the speed a bit."

They danced back to the other side of the room and then around in a full circle. At last the captain released her waist and spun her in a *pirouette.* Sarah laughed.

"See? There's nothing to it," the captain said, still holding her hand.

"I guess that wasn't so bad," Sarah replied.

Captain Sinclair chuckled. "Then you'll have to save a dance for me on Friday night."

Sarah smiled, feeling herself blush.

❧

Days later, on Wednesday, her one day off, Sarah met Richard for lunch.

"I don't expect we'll hear from your father for at least a month," he said, cutting the slice of roast beef on his plate.

Sarah nodded, feeling a bit guilty over not being more excited. Ever since she'd danced with the captain, she was having second thoughts about a courtship with Richard. And yet she had looked forward to this luncheon engagement with him.

"So what are your plans for this afternoon?" Richard asked, bringing Sarah out of her thoughts.

She smiled. "Lina and I are going to do some shopping."

"Uh-oh," Richard said with a teasing gleam in his eyes. "That sounds like trouble."

"You'd better believe it does!" Sarah replied. Then she took her turn at wearing a teasing gleam. "Lina said that it's your birthday next week."

Richard grimaced.

"She said you hate to make a big deal of your birthday. She said it embarrasses you no end."

"Sarah, please don't. . ."

She shrugged in a way that said, "Wait and see."

"I've been known to disappear on my birthday," Richard informed her, cocking an eyebrow.

Again, Sarah shrugged, trying to appear nonchalant.

Richard only chuckled. "Tell you what, Sarah, if it's that important to you, I'll bear the embarrassment of a surprise party."

"Who said anything about a surprise party?"

Richard smiled indulgently. "My mother and Lina try to surprise me every year and every year I guess what they're up to."

"Well, this year will be different," Sarah promised, but that was all she said. Richard would just have to wait and find out for himself!

After lunch, they left the eating establishment and Richard went back to his books. Sarah walked a few blocks to where a row of shops lined the busy street. Lina was already waiting for her. Since school was closed for the summer months, Lina had her days free, though much of her time was spent planning for her upcoming fall wedding.

Strolling down Wisconsin Street, Sarah and Lina peered into shop windows and marveled at the new fashions in the clothing stores. They stopped at the apothecary, and Lina picked up some things for her mother and then they continued their walk.

"What can I buy Richard for his birthday?" Sarah asked after a couple hours of shopping. They had decided on a treat at the ice cream parlor.

"You want to buy Richard a gift?" Lina replied with an incredulous expression. "I don't think that's necessary."

Sarah smiled demurely. "I know. However, Richard has been very good to me since my arrival and I'd like to buy him something special."

Lina laughed softly. "My cousin has ulterior motives, Sarah."

This time Sarah laughed. "Yes, I know." At Lina's second look of surprise, she added, "We've talked about it."

"Sarah. . . !"

She rolled her eyes at Lina's sudden expression of delight. "Don't start making wedding plans or anything."

"Sarah. . . !"

"Oh, will you stop it!"

Lina placed a gloved hand over her mouth to cover her mirth. "Richard has never been interested in any particular young lady," she finally confided, "that's why I'm so tickled. It's a family joke that Richard will be our lifelong bachelor. It started when he was just a boy. He used to tease all the girls and make them cry, so they avoided him—right up until last year, I believe."

They laughed together and Sarah said she could well imagine.

With their ice cream now finished and thoroughly enjoyed, Sarah and Lina left the shop. The day was sunny and bright, and the streets of Milwaukee were busy. The remaining afternoon was spent dawdling in and out of every kind of shop the city had to offer; however, except for a few necessities, Sarah returned to the captain's residence empty-handed. She would have to continue to search for a small birthday gift for Richard.

Up in the quiet of her bedroom that evening, Sarah wrote to her parents. She wanted a letter to follow Richard's so that her parents could make the appropriate decision. She prayed the Holy Spirit would work in their hearts and minds, and out of that, Sarah thought, she too might come to some conclusion regarding her feelings for Richard.

I like him very much, she wrote. *However. . .*

Concerning her heart, there always seemed to be a "however." Sarah thought her parents would not be surprised.

Sarah also thought of writing about the captain and her feelings toward him, although she knew her parents would not approve. Most likely they would make her come home, especially if she confessed to the dancing.

However, part of Sarah—the adventurous part—wanted to dance with him again!

৵

"How long do we have to stand here?" Gabriel whined.

But Sarah just smiled at the boy. He looked so handsome, all dressed up for his father's party, although he'd rather be fishing—and he had been making his feelings known for the last half hour.

"I'm sure your father will dismiss us shortly," Sarah told him.

"I'm sure he's forgotten all about us," Gabriel retorted. "He always forgets. Can't we just leave?"

"No. And let's remember to be respectful at all times. He is your father, whether he forgets or not."

The boy merely shrugged his shoulders.

Libby was tugging on Sarah's skirt. "Miss Sarah! Miss Sarah!"

"Yes, dear," she replied, giving the girl her full attention.

"There's Mrs. Kingsley—the one who came to Aurora's house when we were there. Look!"

Glancing across the crowded ballroom, Sarah spied the

woman. "Don't point your finger that way, Libby," she chided softly. "It's not polite." However, Sarah had to will herself not to openly gape.

The Widow Elise Kingsley was, by far, the belle of the ball. She was a tall, slim brunette, wearing a red silk gown trimmed with black lace. She was dancing with the captain in a most intimate way, and suddenly Sarah felt foolish for ever imagining herself matched with Captain Sinclair. He was much too sophisticated for a little country bumpkin. . .

No! Sarah thought. *I will not succumb to self-pity. I will have to watch and learn. Then I'll be just as sophisticated as anyone else here in this room.*

A half hour passed, then an hour, and Gabriel began to complain again. "Can't we go now? I hate this stuffy party!"

"I believe your father wants you, Michael, and Libby to play your songs on the piano," Sarah replied. "He said you were good enough. He said you wouldn't have to wait until the end of the summer."

"I don't want to play my song," Michael whined. "I'm hungry and tired."

"And I'm hungry, too, Miss Sarah," Libby said with a pout.

"Me, too!" cried little Rachel.

"Father forgot us, anyway," said Gabriel, "so let's go."

Sarah let another half hour pass before deciding that the captain really had forgotten them. His eyes, it seemed, were only on the Widow Kingsley tonight, and Sarah had the odd feeling that the captain was purposely ignoring them. Was it that Mrs. Kingsley didn't like children? Was that why he pretended they didn't exist—because he wanted to impress the rich woman?

Sarah was utterly disgusted with that idea and rather thought they should stay here all night just to annoy Captain Sinclair and let him know they would *not* be ignored! But then she noticed several guests eyeing the tired children speculatively, and she made the decision to leave the party. It wouldn't do, she reasoned, to have the captain's friends think his children were unruly because they were hungry and crabby. They were *children,* after all!

And when they paraded out of the ballroom, the captain didn't even notice.

Down in the kitchen, after the children were done with their supper and cake, Sarah took them for a walk—a "promenade" really, for they were still all dressed up in their Sunday best. Sarah felt a little sorry for them, being ignored by their father. He had said he wanted to "show them off." Then, again, his mind was obviously elsewhere!

Upstairs, preparing the children for bed, Sarah tried to make up for their father's neglect by telling them stories. Bible stories, stories of hope and victory through trusting God. First David and Goliath for the boys, next Deborah for the girls.

"She was the fourth and only female judge of Israel," Sarah told them. "So you see, God uses women, too. And for important tasks."

Libby's eyes were wide with wonder, and Sarah thought even Gabriel looked impressed.

Then once the children were asleep, Sarah retired to her bedroom. She could hear muffled voices from above in the ballroom. She could hear the violins playing beautiful melodies, accompanied by the piano. How tempted she was to join that elite crowd; after all, the captain had invited her. But when Sarah had asked Gretchen if she was going to the party, Gretchen said it was not appropriate for her station. "And it's not appropriate for yours, either, Irish!" she'd concluded.

Sarah had frowned at the remark, but gradually she concluded Gretchen was only reminding her of her proper place. She was only the governess here. She was not a guest.

But someday, Sarah promised herself, *someday I'll have a governess for my children. . .and a big house just like this one. Perhaps the captain will give Richard a promotion. . .a partnership, even! Then I'll be glad to marry him, and we'll never ignore and neglect our children. But we'll teach them proper manners and how to be sophisticated.*

Suddenly, Sarah heard a sound at her window pane. It came again. And again. Ping. Ping. Ping.

"Richard Navis!" she said, opening the window and leaning over the sill. She could see him standing in the yard. "What do you think you're doing?"

Beneath the moonglow, Sarah saw him grin. "I'm throwing gooseberries at your window," he replied. "I was going to throw a brick, but I decided that might be too conspicuous."

Sarah laughed.

"Come down," he beckoned. "Let's go for a stroll."

"I've been for a stroll."

"Then come for another."

"With no chaperon?" she teased.

"I could ask Gretchen," he countered.

"Never mind," Sarah replied.

Richard chuckled.

Grabbing a light wrap, Sarah left her room. She met Richard on the back patio.

"You look lovely tonight," he said with a smile. "I think blue is your color."

"Thank you," Sarah murmured, smoothing the silk of her skirt. It was the best dress she owned. Store bought, too, in Chicago.

Richard held his hand out to her. "Shall we?"

Sarah hesitated for a moment before taking his hand; however, Richard held hers only long enough for her to fall into step beside him. Then he released it, acting the proper gentleman as always.

They strolled down a moon-lit path along the steep cliffs which overlooked Lake Michigan. Overhead, the sky twinkled with stars. *Such a lovely evening,* Sarah thought, inhaling the scent of summer blooms along the walkway. *And to think, God created it all!*

Suddenly, as if divining her thoughts, Richard began quoting the Psalms. " 'When I consider thy heavens, the work of thy fingers, the moon and the stars, which thou hast ordained; What is man, that thou art mindful of him?' " He turned to Sarah. "An awesome thought, isn't it?"

She smiled and nodded. "We have an awesome God." Then, solemnly, she added, "I wish Captain Sinclair would come to know Him."

Richard paused. "I've tried, Sarah," he said at last. "I've explained God's plan of salvation to him and we've talked about it. But I'm afraid the captain refuses to acknowledge that he's a sinner, separated from God, and that the only way to God is through His Son, Jesus Christ. The captain doesn't see—or doesn't want to see—the immediacy of the moment; eternal damnation is but a heartbeat away."

Sarah grew terribly uncomfortable. She hadn't once spoken to the captain about Jesus, even though the Bible so clearly warned in the Book of James that life is "a vapour, that appeareth for a little time, and then vanisheth away."

"We'll keep praying for him," Richard said, taking Sarah's hand and slipping it around his elbow. "All right?"

She nodded, feeling reassured. After all, as her older brother Benjamin liked to say, prayer is what moved mountains and parted seas!

eleven

"I forgot all about Richard's birthday!" Captain Sinclair exclaimed the following week. He had just walked into the kitchen where Sarah and the children were cutting and pasting colored paper together, creating birthday cards for Richard.

"His birfday was really yesterday, Papa," Libby announced, "but we're s'prising him tomorrow with a party. . .right after church." She looked to Sarah for confirmation. "That so, Miss Sarah?"

She smiled. "That's right." Then, turning to the captain, she said, "The party is Sunday and I didn't think you'd mind my taking the children."

"I don't," he stated graciously. "I only wish I would have remembered that Richard's birthday was yesterday." The captain narrowed his gaze at Sarah, feigning irritation. "You should have reminded me."

"Forgive me, Captain," she replied. "I suppose I could have. . . and should have reminded you." *The poor man,* she thought. *He'd forget his head if it weren't attached!*

"Papa, look at my card," Michael said, pushing it into the captain's hand.

"Well, that's a fine one," he replied with pride in his voice, and Sarah recalled how Richard had once said that, despite the captain's shortcomings, he did love his children.

"How 'bout mine, Papa?" Libby asked. "Do you like it?"

Captain Sinclair studied it. "Very good," he finally pronounced.

"Wook! Wook!" cried Rachel.

Captain Sinclair praised his younger daughter for her efforts. "What about yours, Gabriel?" he asked. "Can I see it?"

84

The boy shrugged but handed it to his father.

The captain looked it over. "Why, this is very good." He smiled approvingly. "I should say you're a talented young man."

"You've seen the pictures in his bedroom, haven't you, Captain?" Sarah asked.

He frowned. "No, I haven't."

Sarah turned to Gabriel. "You'll have to show your father your . . .your *gallery*," she said.

"You really want to see my pictures?" the boy asked, looking at his father.

"Of course I want to see them!" the captain replied. Then he tousled Gabriel's hair and went about his way.

"He'll forget," Gabriel murmured as he finished his card for Richard. "He always forgets."

Sarah's heart went out to him. "Perhaps this time your father will remember. We'll pray. . ."

Gabriel looked up at her with questions clouding his light green eyes. But he didn't ask, not yet.

Sarah smiled. *It won't be long,* she thought. Gabriel was interested in God and His ways; and Sarah sensed that Gabriel would soon be ready to accept God's gift of salvation.

The children finished making their birthday cards and then Sarah helped serve their supper. Afterward, she instructed the children individually at the piano.

Then later that evening, after the children were in bed, Sarah encountered Gretchen in the hallway upstairs. "Give this to Mr. Navis!" the housekeeper demanded in her thick German accent.

Sarah examined the basket covered with a checkered linen cloth. "Whatever it is," she said, "it smells delicious."

"It's apple kuchen," Gretchen stated quickly. "Mr. Navis loves my apple kuchen. I made him a dish for his birthday."

Sarah smiled. "That was very thoughtful."

The older woman nodded curtly. "You will give it to Mr. Navis, then?"

The question sounded more like a command, but Sarah nodded anyway. Then she had a question of her own to ask. "Why don't you address Richard by his first name instead of calling him Mr. Navis? I heard him specifically tell you to call him Richard."

"It is not my place, Irish!" Gretchen replied sternly. Sarah's head lifted, for though Gretchen used the word as an insult, Sarah was proud of her heritage. "Mr. Navis has a higher position than I do," Gretchen continued. "Higher than yours, too!"

"But he asked me to call him Richard," Sarah said.

"And I know he has asked you more than that also!"

At the remark, true as it was, Sarah felt her cheeks grow warm with embarrassment. Gretchen, however, didn't seem impressed by her reaction one way or another.

"The children address their grandmother as Aurora," Gretchen continued. "Is that proper? I should say not! But the captain allows it anyhow and it is hardly my place to tell the captain his business."

"Well, somebody has to. . .and you've been in the captain's employment for a very long time. Why, you're practically one of the family!"

"Ha! If a better housekeeper came along, I vould be gone in a minute!" Gretchen exclaimed. She narrowed her gaze at Sarah. "Ve are guaranteed nussing in this lifetime! In minutes, life can change and that vhich ve loved can instantly be gone." She snapped her capable fingers. "Just like that."

Sarah frowned in momentary puzzlement, but then the pieces of Gretchen's past seemed to fall into line. Gretchen Schlyterhaus was angry, hurt, and bitter, Sarah realized, because of her husband's death. And now she was trying desperately to hold onto the only thing she thought she had left: Her position with Captain Sinclair. How obvious it suddenly became!

Sarah's heart began to ache for the older woman. *She needs the Lord Jesus,* she thought. *Jesus is all she'll ever need to get her through this lifetime. . .*

"Vell, in any case, you just make sure to give the apple kuchen to Mr. Navis," Gretchen said at last.

Sarah nodded. But then, as Gretchen began to walk away, she had an idea. "Mrs. Schlyterhaus, would you like to come with us tomorrow? To our worship service and then to the Navises' for Richard's birthday party?"

"Sunday is my day off," the housekeeper replied gruffly over her shoulder.

"Well, yes, I know and that's why I wondered—"

"Of course I vould like to come!" Turning, Gretchen walked the few steps back to Sarah and retrieved the apple kuchen. "I vill give this to Mr. Navis myself!"

With that she stomped off, leaving Sarah gaping in her wake. Then, on an afterthought, Sarah called, "Be ready by eight o'clock. Richard's cousin Lina is coming for us then."

No response; however, Sarah knew Gretchen had heard. Moreover, she was certain that Gretchen would be ready right on time!

❧

Lina and her fiance Timothy arrived in his carriage shortly after breakfast. Sarah made the appropriate introductions and then climbed in after the children. From the front door, Captain Sinclair waved and called, "Have fun." Sarah wished he was coming to church with them, and she prayed that someday he would.

When they arrived at the little country church, Gretchen walked in with the children as Lina held Sarah back by the elbow.

"What happened on Friday?" she whispered.

"Just as you suspected," Sarah whispered back. "Richard asked me to dinner and the theater, but I told him I couldn't go because of. . .of a previous commitment."

Lina giggled. "Oh, that's just grand! Richard probably stewed all weekend!"

Sarah frowned slightly, remembering his expression two days ago. The usual shine in Richard's bright blue eyes had disappeared like the sun behind thunder clouds.

"Lina, I think I hurt his feelings, turning him down on his birthday."

"Well, you can make it up to him today," she replied. "And Richard will laugh about it when he finds out why you turned him down. He loves a good prank. Here he thinks all his friends forgot his birthday, when we've really been planning a party all along. . ."

Sarah smiled, and Lina laughed softly as they walked into the auditorium and found their places. Richard and his parents were seated in the pew in front of them. After she had sat down and settled the children between herself and Lina, with Gretchen at the other end, Richard turned around. He narrowed his gaze speculatively, first at Lina, then at Sarah.

"What are you two up to?" he finally asked. "I saw you whispering outside."

"None of your business," Lina answered.

He glanced at Sarah, who merely shrugged. Then, after giving her an I-know-that-you're-up-to-something look, Richard turned back around. Sarah and Lina exchanged amused and knowing smiles.

The morning worship service began with hymns of praise. Sarah watched curiously as Gretchen opened the hymnal and followed along. She didn't sing, although she seemed to be looking at the words. Then it occurred to Sarah that perhaps Mrs. Schlyterhaus couldn't read English. She was, after all, from Germany. Returning her eyes to her own song book now, Sarah decided she would have to do something about that. She would ask Richard about getting a German hymnal.

After the service, Sarah ushered the Sinclair children outside to the waiting carriage. Gretchen suggested that she keep the two little girls with her and ride with Lina and Timothy while Sarah take the boys and ride with Richard and his parents.

"*Ve* will not be so cramped," she added, fanning herself with her white gloves.

Sarah nodded and had to agree that it was certainly a hot day!

Smiling, Richard helped Sarah up into the wagon, after which he boosted the two boys into the back. He had already helped his father into the wagon, which was no simple task because of Marty Navis's paralyzed legs. However, Sarah had noticed that Mr. Navis helped himself by using his arms which, since his accident, had grown thick and muscular—a result of having to lift his own weight.

"How did you manage to get Gretchen to church this morning, Sarah?" Richard asked, climbing into the wagon now.

She shrugged. "I just invited her."

"Well, I've been inviting her for years!" Richard exclaimed. "So has my mother."

"Really?" The idea gave Sarah pause. "Well, perhaps Mrs. Schlyterhaus doesn't dislike me after all," she said hopefully.

Richard grinned. "I'd wager that it's impossible to dislike you, Sarah." He chuckled. "Why, you've even managed to win Gabriel and Michael, and they disliked every governess the captain ever hired!"

"Yes, so I've gathered," Sarah replied, smiling all the while. "Those two can be rascals!" She looked into the back of the wagon and found the boys preoccupied with something Michael was holding in his palm. A bug, no doubt.

"Well, I'm so pleased you're spending Sundays with us, Sarah," Mrs. Navis said, sitting beside her. The two men were in front, Richard with the reins.

"I am also pleased, Sarah," Richard said. Then he looked over his shoulder, wearing a mischievous smile, and Sarah shook her head at him.

However, she enjoyed Richard's humor more than she cared to admit, and she was very glad to spend Sundays with him and his family. The Navises made her feel right at home with their relaxed and unpretentious ways. They weren't out to impress her or win her; they just loved her—Richard's feelings being quite different from his parents', of course. In any case, Sarah knew they were genuine, earthy folks around whom she could freely share her heart and enjoy the goodness of the Lord.

"Sometimes I get homesick when I spend time with your family," she confided to Richard later as they took a walk around the potato field. The stroll was actually a diversion of sorts, as Lina and Mrs. Navis wanted to get things in order for Richard's surprise birthday party—without him around.

Richard smiled at her statement. "What is it exactly that makes you homesick?"

"Well, sometimes all the activity at your house on Sundays reminds me of home in Missouri. Ben and Valerie bring their two little boys. . ." Sarah shrugged, feeling misty-eyed all of a sudden.

"I thought you were glad to be away from Missouri."

"I am, I guess. I mean, for the most part, yes, I'm glad to be on my own. I value my independence. I just miss my family sometimes."

Walking around the property, they ended up on the far side of the apple orchard.

"So, you value your independence, do you?" Richard asked rhetorically as they sat down beneath a large tree.

Sarah nodded and, reaching up, she removed her bonnet and then patted several pins back into place.

Richard was chuckling softly. "Sarah, how independent do you really think you are? You don't have to cook, launder clothes, clean house, concern yourself with finances, a roof over your head, clothes on your back. . ."

"I am, too, concerned about the clothes on my back!" she teased.

Richard laughed. "You know what I mean. Everyone takes care of you. The captain. Gretchen. Isabelle. Me."

"Yes, I know what you mean," Sarah conceded. "And that's exactly what I love about my independence. I'm independent of all those horrible tasks!" She laughed merrily, knowing it was the truth, but unwilling to change it in any way. She wanted to be pampered, and she wanted to be rich! "But I do work for my living, let me remind you. Taking care of four children isn't exactly complete luxury."

Richard shrugged. "Sarah," he began after a few pensive moments, "you're not independent. You're spoiled!"

She turned sharply, studying his face. She couldn't tell if Richard was teasing or if he'd meant that last remark. In any case, Sarah thought she deserved to be a little spoiled. Hadn't she worked—and worked hard!—back in Missouri? She knew very well what it was like to do all those things Richard had mentioned. . .and then some! It wasn't until she'd met her sister-in-law Valerie that she'd begun to hunger for a different way of life. The kind of life Valerie had had as a socialite in a big city like New Orleans before she married Benjamin. And, although Valerie maintained that she was happier in love and doing all those mundane household chores, Sarah had grown tired of them and had longed to be on her own. And now she was!

Richard suddenly stood and held his hand out to Sarah. She took it and he pulled her to her feet.

"I'm going to have to do some serious praying," he told her with just a hint of a grin. He still held onto her hand.

Then, before Sarah could inquire over his need for "serious prayer," Richard's grin faded and he pulled her into his arms and kissed her.

Sarah's first impulse was to push him away, but curiosity allowed her to relax. As if sensing her acquiescence, Richard deepened his kiss until Sarah felt herself responding.

Finally, Richard pulled himself away. His deep blue eyes held such tenderness that Sarah thought she might like to drown in them. Slipping her arms around Richard's neck, she leaned forward for another sweet kiss.

"No more, Sarah," he said hoarsely, pushing her arms away gently. "I was wrong to even initiate the first." He sighed, momentarily closing his eyes in what seemed a mixture of remorse and agony. "Please forgive me." Looking at her once more, he added, "I just love you so much. . .I couldn't help it."

Feeling as though her senses had now returned, Sarah nodded. "I need to ask your forgiveness, too, Richard. I am as much to blame; I could have put a stop to it right away."

Several long and tense moments passed. Then Richard smiled broadly. "That was the best birthday present I'll get today!" he declared with a sheepish expression.

"Whatever do you mean, Richard Navis?" Sarah asked, batting her lashes innocently.

"I mean. . .out of all the presents I'll receive today at my *surprise party,* that was the best!"

Sarah tried to play dumb, but she couldn't quite pull it off. "You're incorrigible, Richard!" she exclaimed at last. "You knew all along, didn't you?"

"Not quite, but I suspected it," he replied with a laugh. Then he took her hand. "Come along," he said, leading her out of the apple orchard and toward the house, "I believe it's party time!"

twelve

Richard watched as his uncle's carriage pulled out of the circle drive, heading toward Lisbon Plank Road. The evening sun was just beginning to set, casting long shadows across the lawn. Richard waved and Sarah waved back from where she was sitting next to Lina, holding Rachel on her lap.

The afternoon had been delightful, and Richard knew he would treasure the memory of it for a long, long time. Gretchen's gift would certainly be a delicious reminder; the handkerchief, on which Bethany had embroidered his initials, would be useful; and Lina and Tim's generous birthday gift of two theater tickets was more than appreciated. However, Sarah's gift—the handsome set of pens—troubled Richard. A farmer would have no use for pens of that magnitude! Sleek and black, trimmed with gold, they must have cost Sarah plenty. Moreover, Sarah had said she'd searched and searched for the "perfect birthday gift."

"Did you tell her, son?"

Richard turned to find that his father had wheeled his chair onto the large front porch.

"Did you tell her about the decision you made last night?"

Slowly, Richard shook his head.

"I thought you would have taken the time while you two strolled this afternoon."

"I should have, Pops," he admitted. Instead, he had made the mistake of kissing Sarah. He was sorry, and he'd asked God's forgiveness. After all, Sarah didn't belong to him. . .yet.

Marty Navis sighed deeply. "Well, if you want to change your mind—"

"I don't. I won't," Richard stated. "I want to work this farm, Pops. I want to get married and live here. . .and raise my family here."

His father laughed. "Well, I know you've always loved the farm, Richard, but to hear you talk about marriage. . ." He laughed once more. "Until you met that pretty little gal from Missouri, you were singing a bachelor-for-life tune."

Richard grinned. "I guess that's right, Pops."

Marty squinted speculatively. "Do you think Miss Sarah will want the same? She seems awfully city-minded. Told me she was tired of country living and she told your mother that she likes being in the captain's fancy house."

Richard sighed. He had suspected that was how Sarah felt, and yet he was praying she'd come to love him enough to live anywhere on God's green earth. . .including his farm!

"I don't know, Pops." Richard sat in a porch chair next to his father's wheel chair. "I suppose we'll just have to see."

"It may be, son, that you'll have to choose—this farm, or Sarah." His father looked him square in the eye. "Then what?"

Richard didn't answer right away, thinking the question through. Finally he said, "Pops, I refuse to decide on one or the other. I want Sarah for my wife, and I want this farm. And I believe, because I've talked to Him about it, that God intends to bless me with both."

Marty grinned. "You claim a passage of scripture to support that?"

Richard matched his smile. "Didn't have to claim it. God gave it. Psalm hundred and twenty-six, verses five and six: 'They that sow in tears shall reap in joy. He that goeth forth and weepeth, bearing precious seed, shall doubtless come again with rejoicing, bringing his sheaves with him.'" Looking across the yard and the apple orchard, Richard's gaze stopped at the small pond. "A good amount of my sweat and an equal amount of my tears may have to be shed, Pops," he said. "But, with God as my witness, I'm going to work this land as best I'm able. . .and I'm going to marry Sarah McCabe!"

℘

The month of July continued, hot and sticky, and finally a letter from Reverend McCabe arrived. Tim delivered it to the captain's shop, wearing a grin.

"Open it," he instructed.

Richard nodded and swallowed hard as he tore into the envelope and read the letter.

> *Dear Mr. Navis (May I call you Richard?):*
> *My wife and I were quite surprised by your letter. The fact that Sarah gave you consent to post it, coupled by her letter which told us of your interest as well, astounded us no end!*
> *But, having recovered from the shock, I do hereby give you my permission to court Sarah. I do, however, expect her to return to Chicago and to her teaching position in the fall. The two of you will just have to correspond until the Christmas holiday. At that time, I want Sarah to return home, here to Missouri, but she may bring you and your parents along.*
> *My wife and I are very anxious to meet you, Richard. We think it'll be a very, merry Christmas, indeed!*

Smiling, Richard looked up. "Thank You, Jesus!" he shouted, causing several of his coworkers to cast curious looks in his direction. But Richard was too happy to care what others thought. Looking at Tim, he said, "The courtship of Sarah McCabe has just begun!"

"Amen!" Tim declared.

That very evening, Richard read the letter to Sarah as they

walked along the cliffs. He smiled all the while. Sarah, however, merely rolled her eyes in embarrassment.

"You've done it now, Richard Navis," she told him, looking a bit worried. "My father will interrogate you the entire Christmas holiday and so will my brothers."

"I'm not concerned, Sarah," he replied, chuckling.

"You ought to be," she murmured.

Richard just chuckled all the harder. Then, folding Reverend McCabe's letter, he tucked it back in his shirt pocket. Next he took Sarah's hand and wrapped it around his elbow. As they strolled amicably toward the downtown area, a deep gnawing conviction settled upon Richard. He had to tell Sarah about his decision to farm. . .and it seemed the Lord was prompting him to be honest with her right now.

"Sarah, let's sit and talk a while." He nodded toward a bench on the walk which overlooked Lake Michigan.

"What do you want to talk about?" Sarah asked as they sat down. A cool breeze was blowing off the lake and she thought it felt wonderful after the heat of the day. Having taken the children to their swimming lessons, taught them their piano lessons, then seen to their supper and baths, Sarah felt wilted. However, this walk by the lake was doing wonders for her disposition.

Richard cleared his throat. "Sarah, you know I'm very pleased that your father has given me permission to court you."

Nodding, she smiled. She was glad he was pleased.

"Now, let's just imagine for a moment that you fall madly in love with me and we get married."

Sarah sighed dramatically. "Richard, I'm far too tired to try my imagination that way." She laughed.

He gave her a little smile. "I'm trying to be serious, here."

She sobered.

"I'm trying to tell you something on my heart, Sarah."

"Oh, all right. Go ahead."

Again, Richard cleared his throat. "So, let's say that we get married," he continued. "Now, where do you see us making our home?"

Sarah thought a moment and then shrugged. "Right here in Milwaukee, I suppose."

Richard nodded. "Yes, that's good. I had thought the same." He frowned in momentary consternation before continuing. "Sarah, I guess I should come right out and tell you. . ." He looked up at her and took one of her hands, sandwiching it between both of his. "The transfer has been legally made—I've purchased my father's home and I plan to farm the land. I'm going to give my notice to Captain Sinclair tomorrow, but I wanted you to know first. When my service is up, which will be at the end of August, I will resign and take up farming full time."

"What?" Sarah's jaw dropped at the incredible news. "A farmer? You are planning to be a farmer?"

Richard didn't flinch. "Yes, I am."

"But you have such a promising future with the captain!"

"Perhaps in a sense, yes. But I'm unhappy in my current position and I've known for quite some time now that it's not for me."

Sarah stood and was thoughtful for several long minutes as she gazed out over the lake. "So what you're telling me is. . .if I marry you, Richard, I will be a farmer's wife."

"That's right."

"No! Never!" Sarah declared, spinning around to face him. "I care for you, Richard, but not *that* much."

Richard swallowed his sudden hurt. "Sarah, please, be reasonable."

"I am being reasonable!"

"Then let's talk this matter over."

"No. And you can forget about courting me."

"Sarah!"

"You may, however, call on me if you change your mind," she said, turning and walking away. Then over her shoulder, she added, "If I wanted to marry a farmer, I could have stayed in Missouri!"

Sarah's pointed words cut into Richard's heart. Too hurt and stunned to even follow her back to the captain's home, he let Sarah walk home alone.

Sitting back down on the bench, Richard told himself that he shouldn't be surprised by Sarah's reaction. He had sensed that she wouldn't like his news. . .at first. But she enjoyed her Sundays on the farm; Richard had been sure that Sarah would at least consider the idea of marrying him and living there with him.

Well, perhaps she'll have a change of heart, he thought.

❧

Entering the captain's home, Sarah was thinking along the same lines, except she hoped Richard was the one who would have the change of heart. Things had been going so well. In fact, sometimes Sarah thought she even loved Richard. But marry a farmer? No! No! No!

As she came around the back stairwell, someone caught her arm. Turning suddenly, she found herself looking up at Captain Sinclair.

He donned an amused little smile. "Why on earth are you frowning so? You're lucky Aurora didn't see you. She'd give you an hour's lecture on how a frown ages a young lady's face!"

Sarah realized the captain was teasing her. She forced a smile. "Forgive me, sir, but I've just heard some disturbing news."

The captain frowned. "And what is that?"

Gently pulling her arm free of his grasp, Sarah shrugged helplessly. "I believe you'll hear it tomorrow, Captain."

His dark gaze narrowed as he considered her with pursed lips. *Now why can't Richard be more like the captain?* Sarah wondered as she looked into his handsome face. *Why can't Richard be more ambitious, business minded, serious, and mature?*

"Sarah, tell me what you've heard."

"I'm afraid I can't, Captain Sinclair."

"I see." He folded his arms across his chest. "Has this anything to do with my steward, Richard Navis, with whom you have been spending a good deal of time lately?"

Sarah didn't need a looking glass to know she was blushing profusely. Her cheeks were aflame, and Sarah could feel the heat to the tip of her nose.

The captain smiled. "By your expression, I can tell that it does. May I assume that your short affair with him is now over?"

"Affair?" Sarah wondered if that's what sophisticated people termed a courtship: An "affair."

"Sarah, my dear," the captain continued, "I could have saved both of you time and heartache—that is, I could have saved Richard the heartache and you the time. You are hardly a match for him. I can tell. You want more from this life than Richard could ever give you."

He paused, putting a booted foot up on a stair and leaning a powerful-looking forearm against his leg. Sarah backed away from him against the wall.

Captain Sinclair considered her long and hard with a slight smile curving his handsome mouth. "If I weren't such a gentleman, Sarah, and you weren't quite so young, I should say I'd like to kiss you."

Her eyes widened in surprise and her heart fairly flew into her throat.

"Moreover," the captain continued, "I expect that you'd enjoy it."

"Captain Sinclair!" she gasped, feeling horrified now. "I am not that kind of a. . .a. . ."

"Of course you're not," he agreed. "And I didn't mean to imply that you are anything less than a proper young woman. However, you have a passionate nature, Sarah, and that's quite obvious."

"Oh, dear!" she exclaimed, wondering what her mother would say if she discovered this "passionate nature." Then Sarah recalled how she had enjoyed Richard's kiss, and the memory added a feeling of shame to her current discomfort.

But Captain Sinclair just laughed. "Sarah, what I mean is that you would never be happy with a man like Richard Navis. He's too. . .too dependable. You want to live life to its fullest. You want adventure and the finer things this world has to offer. Richard, on the other hand, could care less for finery and, matched with him, you would be miserable. And so would he, because he could never please you."

Sarah thought the captain had spoken exactly what was in her heart, and yet, once verbalized, the words made her feel like a haughty and shallow person. And that, Sarah decided, was more disturbing than the captain's remark about how he'd like to kiss her.

However, she was unwilling to pursue these conflicting emotions. In a swirl of skirts, Sarah turned and ran up the stairs, leaving the captain chuckling in her wake.

thirteen

For the next few days, Richard pursued Sarah in spite of the hurtful words she had thrown at him. He couldn't believe she really meant them, nor was he about to give up, not yet. He even managed to overcome the captain's words of discouragement.

"Why don't you forget this farm idea?" the captain asked on a suggestive note. "Perhaps Sarah would consider you then. You'd have a good future working for me; you would be successful and could financially afford a young woman like Sarah McCabe. She desires fine things and a life in the city. To tell you the truth, I can't blame her."

Richard gritted his teeth. "Money isn't everything, Captain. I can't buy Sarah. . .like you can't buy your way to heaven."

"Come now, Richard, I'm not talking about buying anyone or anything. I'm talking about a way of life. A comfortable way of life."

"I know what you're talking about," Richard said, softening his tone, "and I thank you for your concern. But either Sarah loves me for what I am or she doesn't love me at all!"

Captain Sinclair shook his head sadly. "Such a romantic."

Richard, however, didn't think he was any more romantic than any other man. He was just in love. . .in love with Sarah McCabe. What's more, he had a feeling that, worldly things aside, she loved him, too. So Richard prayed often and fervently, desperately wanting God's will for both their lives.

❧

Sarah, on the other hand, was both amazed and irritated at Richard's perseverance. She allowed him a few visits, but finally refused him altogether until, at last, he agreed to put some distance between them.

"So you can come to your senses," Richard said.

"So you can come to yours!" Sarah retorted.

And for the weeks following, as the hot summer days passed into the sultry month of August, Richard didn't come around. Likewise, Sarah and the children refrained from going to the Navises' farm on Sunday afternoons. However, they continued to attend church services since Lina and Timothy insisted upon driving them, despite Sarah and Richard's "misunderstanding," as Lina called it. And there, at church, Sarah caught glimpses of Richard, although they only exchanged polite greetings.

The only problem was, now that Richard had given Sarah her way, she was miserable! She found herself remembering his laughter and how blue his eyes would get when he was up to some kind of mischief. She thought her days were longer and more tedious now, without Richard spicing them up. Yes, she missed him; however, she didn't know what to do about it. She wished they could at least be friends, but Richard said he didn't want to be her friend; he wanted to be her husband! Then, to make matters worse, each week the children begged to go to the farm after church, and each week Sarah had to tell them, "No."

"But why?" Gabriel cried this week—just as he had last week. "Why can't we go to the Navises' farm?"

"Gabriel, I have explained this to you already," Sarah said sternly as she pulled on one white glove and then the other. "We no longer have a standing invitation there."

"But Mr. Navis said we were invited if you'd say yes!" Michael declared.

"I will not say yes to Mr. Navis's offer," Sarah replied, knowing that the *offer* went well beyond a visit to the farm. And yet she too missed Sunday afternoons with the Navis family—and yes, with Richard, too! *If only he weren't so intent upon being a farmer,* she mused with a deep frown marring her brow.

"Please, Sarah," Gabriel continued to plead, "it's the only thing that makes me happy—going to that farm on Sunday afternoons."

Sarah swung around from where she had been examining her appearance in the foyer's looking glass. "Why, Gabriel," she said, astounded, "we do plenty of fun things."

"But they're not like being on the farm."

Considering the boy, Sarah tilted her head. "Why not?"

"'Cuz I'm free there," Gabriel replied simply. "It's not like here, or at Aurora's house. I'm not free here or there. I have to sit up straight and not slurp my soup and I have to wear fancy jackets that make me feel sweaty. But on the farm, I can just be me, and if I accidentally slurp my soup, nobody cares."

Sarah sighed, thinking the whole matter trivial. "Nobody cares here either, Gabe, if you accidentally slurp your soup—"

"You don't understand!" he shouted. "You're just like them! My father. . .and Aurora!"

"Gabriel?"

"I thought you were different!" With that, he turned on his heel and ran up the front staircase just as the captain entered the foyer.

"What's going on here?" he asked, giving Sarah a quizzical look.

Quickly, she scooted Michael, Libby, and Rachel onto the front porch to wait for Lina and Tim.

"It was nothing, Captain. Really."

"But the shouting—was that Gabriel?"

Sarah hesitated in her reply. She didn't want to get the boy in trouble with his father.

"Sarah? Was Gabriel shouting at you?"

"Actually, we were discussing something that Gabriel feels very strongly about, sir. But I'll fetch him now and everything will be fine."

Forgetting herself, as she often did, Sarah ran up the front stairs after Gabriel. She passed Gretchen in the upstairs hallway.

"Vill you ever learn to use the servants' stairvell?" the house-keeper cried.

"Yes, ma'am, I will," Sarah promised over her shoulder. "I'll try not to forget again."

Gretchen clucked her tongue, but said no more. Ever since Sarah had purchased a German hymnal for her, Gretchen's outward disdain had faded somewhat, though she'd made the remark that "only the Irish can get away vith murder." Gretchen had, of course, been referring to Captain Sinclair's obvious favoritism toward Sarah. He rarely refused any of her requests; however, Sarah knew Gretchen's remark went back to the time when her husband had been killed in the German-Irish riots, and she prayed that Gretchen would soon learn to forgive. Only then would the Lord be able to heal her heart.

Sarah reached Gabriel's bedroom and knocked on the door. "Come on, Gabe," she called, "open up. Everyone is ready for church. Even Mrs. Schlyterhaus."

Slowly, the door opened, and Sarah had to force herself not to gasp when she saw Gabriel's tear-streaked face. The sight was enough to bring tears to her own eyes, for Gabriel Sinclair was not a boy easily moved to emotion.

"It's that important to you?" she asked him softly. "Visiting the farm?"

Gabriel replied with a noncommittal shrug.

"You know," Sarah began, "freedom really starts in the heart of a person. It's not a place. And only Jesus can make us free."

Gabriel shook his head. "You don't understand. I can't explain it. . .it's like I'm happy there at the farm. But I'm not happy here."

"Perhaps that's because the Navis family knows Jesus and you can sense that. Perhaps the reason you experience happiness there is because you're experiencing the Navises' freedom. Freedom from sin and guilt and shame—because of what Jesus did on the cross."

Again, Gabriel shrugged.

"And if you ask Jesus to forgive you for your sins and if you ask Him into your heart," Sarah told Gabriel, "then I believe you'll find happiness anywhere."

Gabriel thought a moment. "Have you asked Jesus into your heart?" he finally asked.

Sarah nodded. "Jesus saved me when I was a little girl."

"Then how come you can't be happy anywhere?" he countered. "How come you can't be happy on a farm?"

Sarah gasped. "Why, Gabriel! How in the world—"

"I heard you," he continued. "I heard you talking to Miss Lina. You said you couldn't possibly marry Mr. Navis 'cuz you'd never be happy on a farm."

Sarah drew back her chin. "I was speaking of a different kind of happiness!" she declared, sounding defensive to her own ears. "And you can't understand because you're a child. Now, come along, Gabriel, we're going to church!"

Sarah marched back down the hallway and then down the front staircase. At the bottom, she found Captain Sinclair leaning against the banister, smiling.

"Oh, my, I forgot again," she murmured.

The captain chuckled. "It's a good thing Gretchen didn't see you. . .again. I escorted her out to the carriage and saved you another tongue lashing!"

Sarah smiled. "I'm very grateful, Captain."

"And what about Gabriel?"

"He's coming, sir."

"Very good."

"And what about you, Captain?" Sarah asked, suddenly feeling bold. "Will you come to church with us today?"

He laughed heartily. "I think not, my dear. I am not interested in hearing anything a long-winded preacher has to say." Looping Sarah's gloved hand around his elbow, Captain Sinclair ushered her toward the front door. "Besides, I won't hear anything at your church that Richard hasn't already told me. Sitting in a pew won't do me a bit of good!"

"But, Captain—"

"Now, Sarah," he chided her gently, "I'll hear no more of it. The fact is, I can't go to church. . .even if I wanted to. I have an engagement. I'm taking Elise Kingsley, Aurora, and her escort, John St. Martin, on a lake excursion today. We'll set sail mid-morning. Aurora has already sent a messenger so I won't forget."

Captain Sinclair suddenly grinned. "Why don't you and the children join us, Sarah? Come sailing with me out on beautiful Lake Michigan instead of perspiring in a stuffy chapel. It'll be so refreshing. . .sailing does a body wonders. And Aurora is very fond of you. She says you have 'possibilities.' And the boys can fish. What do you say?"

Sarah faltered, but only momentarily. "Oh, no, Captain," she replied, though she was sorely tempted. She wondered what it would be like to go on a lake excursion with a man like Captain Kyle Sinclair and his affluent friends.

"Are you certain, Sarah?" the captain asked with a handsome grin. "You look like you might be persuaded—"

"Not at all!" she said with determination this time. "This is the Lord's day and He has commanded that we set it aside to worship Him."

"Worship your God out on the lake," the captain replied suggestively.

Sarah swallowed down her desire to go with him as well as her timidness to tell him why she couldn't. *Help me, Lord,* she pleaded quickly and silently. Then to the captain she said, "Please forgive me if I'm out of line, but you and your friends, Captain, are not believers, nor do you care to be. You said as much yourself. Moreover, I highly doubt that your excursion will be conducive to worshipping God Almighty!"

A slow, sardonic grin curved the captain's mouth. "You've got a point there, my dear Sarah." Then he chuckled. "Very well. You and the children go to church. I suppose it is better for them."

Sarah nodded her agreement as Gabriel came down the stairs, all shined up and ready to go. Then the captain walked Sarah out to the awaiting carriage.

"I'm going to pray for you, Captain Sinclair," she stated in a final act of daring.

He smiled wryly. "And I shall think of you, dear Sarah, while I'm cooling myself in the middle of Lake Michigan with two of the wealthiest people in Milwaukee: Elise Kingsley and John St. Martin."

He saluted her then, and Sarah knew he was mocking her. But as he chuckled and helped her up into the carriage, Sarah promised herself that she wouldn't give up praying for Captain Sinclair's salvation.

≥

When the carriage pulled onto the dusty gravel drive in front of the little church, Sarah was hot, sticky, and withered feeling. The children, too, were miserable, and Sarah half wished she had taken the captain's offer of a lake excursion. Cool water. . .how refreshing it would feel. Unfortunately, the only available supply was not that of a vast body of water, but of a little spring-fed well.

Sarah led the children around back to the pump where they splashed their faces and took long, thirst-quenching gulps. Then, after she took a turn herself, Sarah gathered the children and together they entered the church building. Richard was standing at the doorway; he appeared to be waiting for them, and a little thrill passed through Sarah. He looked so handsome in his fashionable matching suit, and Sarah tumultuously decided it wasn't fair that a farmer should look so good!

"Good morning, Richard," she said, smiling as the children descended upon him.

He lifted Rachel into his arms, removing her clutching fingers from his knees. "Hello, Sarah," he returned warmly. "I saw Gretchen come in behind Lina and Tim, but I didn't see you or the children."

"The heat slowed us down, I'm afraid."

Richard grinned. "Well, it got me worried. . .that is, concerned.

I think 'worry' might be a sin."

Sarah smiled at the glib remark and, despite the "distance" she had agreed to—even insisted upon—she couldn't help but feel cheered just seeing Richard again. *Oh, why, can't I just fall in love with him and be done with it?* she wondered. *If only Richard's ambition weren't farming. If only he were more like Captain Sinclair. . .*

They walked into the cool auditorium and sat down in the back pew. Sarah had been taking this same spot for weeks in case Rachel got fussy during the services, but, since they had arrived early today, the children were allowed to get the talking and squirming out of their systems while the rest of the congregation was scattered about chatting.

"How have you been, Richard? I haven't spoken more than three sentences to you in weeks," Sarah ventured. "How are your parents?"

Richard shifted in his place beside her. He seemed suddenly uncomfortable. "Sarah, I think. . .well, I mean, I need to talk to you about something. . ."

At that exact moment, Bethany Stafford plopped down excitedly in the next pew in front of them. "Hello, Sarah," she said with a brilliant smile, causing Sarah to wonder why she'd ever thought Bethany to be a plain young woman. Today her soft brown hair was carefully pulled back and her cheeks were flushed prettily. "Look, Sarah!" she said, indicating an ivory locket which hung on a delicate golden chain around her neck. "I'm betrothed!"

"Betrothed?" For a moment Sarah thought all the breath had left her lungs, she was so stunned. Bethany? Bethany was to marry . . .marry. . .*Richard*? Was that why he was so suddenly uncomfortable acting just now?

Then Richard began to chuckle. "Beth, you may want to inform Sarah who it is you're betrothed to before she faints dead away!"

Bethany looked a bit embarrassed. "Oh, yes, of course. . .I'm betrothed to Lionel Barnes. Mr. Timothy Barnes' younger brother. Remember him, Sarah? We all went to the theater together."

Sarah nodded. She remembered Lionel, all right.

"My parents have insisted that we wait for at least a year to get married," Bethany babbled happily. "Papa says Lionel is a good fellow, but he's got some rough edges that need smoothing."

"I see," Sarah breathed. At least Bethany wasn't marrying Richard, although her betrothal to Lionel did seem a bit hasty. On the other hand, a year's time would surely tell.

Richard laughed as Bethany stood up to show her locket to another friend. "You should have seen your face, Sarah," he told her. "Could have knocked you over with a feather after Bethany announced her betrothal!"

"Oh, quiet," Sarah replied irritably, and she wished she had done better at hiding her reaction.

"You know what I think?" Richard whispered, leaning over slightly. "I think you're in love with me, and I think you ought to do yourself—and me—a favor and admit it!"

"Go sit somewhere else," Sarah retorted. "I've got enough to manage with the captain's children, let alone you!"

Richard sobered. "Do you really want me to go, Sarah? Or has your pride been wounded?"

She frowned. "My pride?"

"Yes, your pride. You're full of it."

"Richard! How dare you say such a thing?" she hissed at him. "First you say I'm spoiled and now you say I'm prideful. . .how can you say you. . .you love me if you really think I possess those horrible qualities?"

He ignored the question. "Do I go? Or do I stay?"

Sarah folded her arms stubbornly. How much like her brother Luke Richard seemed at times. Both men were so blunt and ruthless with their words. Didn't Richard know how he hurt her when he called her those things—spoiled and prideful?

"Sarah? I'm waiting for an answer. Shall I go?"

She didn't reply, but she didn't want Richard to sit somewhere else either. Not really. Sarah had missed him, it was true. And perhaps she did love him. But to admit that would mean spending the rest of her life on a farm.

A farm! No! No! No! And, as far as pride was concerned, Sarah didn't think she was behaving in a prideful manner. She had dreams, that was all. Ambitions. Why couldn't Richard understand that?

Then slowly, and without another word, Richard got up from the pew and walked forward to where his parents were sitting. Sarah watched as they moved to make room for him, and then Richard sat down. Smoothing her skirt, Sarah willed back the tears which threatened; she had made her decision and now she had to live with it.

fourteen

Sarah stood in the shade by the wooden wagon, waiting for Lina and Tim and the captain's children. The worship service had ended and now many of the congregation, including Lina and Tim, were partaking in some fellowship. The Sinclair children, along with several others, were running about in the adjacent field and splashing in the nearby small stream. Sarah was glad she had remembered to pack the children's play clothes. Now they would be much cooler on the ride back home.

She sighed as a faint waft touched her cheek, causing her to long for much more. *Oh, for a hearty breeze,* she thought, *I think I'd do anything, Lord,* she prayed now, looking skyward. *Please send just a bit of a wind. . .*

Right then Richard came strolling toward her. He looked as uncomfortable as she felt, though he had long since removed his suit jacket. But on his face he wore a mischievous grin, and Sarah was irked that he could smile while she felt so hot and miserable.

Then she thought of the captain and his friends, cool and comfortable and sailing away on Lake Michigan. She nearly groaned aloud.

"Wanning by the wagon, are you, Sarah, my lovely?"

She lifted a derisive brow in reply. "Can you really be speaking to me? Someone so *spoiled* and *prideful.*"

Richard shrugged. "Can't seem to stay away, I guess."

Sarah didn't reply, but removed her gloves and then used them to fan herself. The heat didn't leave much room for propriety. The gloves were off now and, as soon as they left the church yard, Sarah was determined to remove her waist jacket with its stylish three-quarter length sleeves.

111

"The heat is ghastly, isn't it?"

Sarah nodded. "Seems we agree on that much, anyway."

Richard chuckled. Then, for a few moments, neither of them spoke. Richard leaned against the wagon beside her. "Sarah, I wrote to your father again." All traces of humor were gone from his face now. "I told him of the problems we've been experiencing during our, uh, courtship."

Sarah didn't know what to say to that. Her family, of course, would not be surprised. Disappointed, perhaps, but not surprised.

"You do realize," Richard continued, "that your father wants you to return to your teaching position in September. That's two weeks away."

"Yes, I realize that."

Richard turned sideways now to face Sarah. He propped his elbow on the side of the wagon. He wished he could force her into changing her mind, but he knew he couldn't. Only God could change Sarah's heart. But once she left for Chicago, Richard feared he'd lose her forever.

"I wonder," he said slowly, "if you and the children would like to come out to the farm today. The children will have a wonderful time. They can play in the pond. And we can watch them from the front porch. It's shaded for most of the day and stays nice and cool."

"I. . .I don't know, Richard—"

"My parents would love to have you visit again."

"Your parents," Sarah said, sounding dejected, "must think I'm a shrew."

Richard laughed. "Hardly."

"Spoiled and prideful," she shot at him with a twinkle in her sky-blue eyes.

Richard, of course, had to bite. "Hmm. . .well, 'spoiled' and 'prideful' might describe any one of us at any given time. And then, of course, there's always God's grace to cover it. . .if we realize our sin and confess it." Richard lifted encouraging brows.

Sarah appeared to consider what he said, but then suddenly folded her arms stubbornly. "Despite any feelings I may have for you, Richard, I don't want to live on a farm!" she said abruptly.

"And I don't want to argue with you. It's much too hot."

She turned suddenly and now they stood face-to-face. "Why don't you change your mind, Richard? I've missed you so! We have such fun together. Can't we just put all this strife behind us? I mean, why must it be your way or my way? Can't we just come to some sort of compromise?"

Looking down at her earnest, pleading face, Richard was tempted, and he thought perhaps he understood now how Adam felt in the Garden.

"Please, Richard," Sarah cajoled sweetly, and Richard thought his very heart would melt—and not from the heat of the day, either.

However, he knew that he could not compromise on what he felt certain was the will of God for his life. He was called to plow and plant; he was called to be a farmer.

"Sarah, come to the farm today," Richard told her. "We'll talk. We'll get some things settled between us once and for all. I promise."

She fretted over her lower lip for a good minute as they both stood gazing at each other.

"We don't have much time left," Richard reminded her. "It'll be more difficult to communicate once you're back in Chicago."

Finally Sarah nodded. "All right. I'll come to the farm today."

❧

Gabriel was ecstatic that they were going to the Navises' farm, and his enthusiasm spilled over onto the other children. They skipped and hopped back to the wagon, acting as if the temperature weren't ninety degrees.

Lina and Tim were pleased, too, as they accepted an invitation from the Navises for the afternoon. They would then drive Sarah and the children back to the captain's home later in the evening.

Gretchen was invited as well, but declined and found a way back to town in a landau with a gentleman who owned a sausage shop. He was German, too, and a butcher by trade. His wife had died long ago, and now he lived with his widowed sister above the shop. Richard said he was a fine man and that Gretchen was in good company.

Sarah nodded as he helped her into Tim's buckboard. Minutes later, they were on their way.

"I do hope you and Richard can come to terms about your relationship," Lina remarked as they rode to the Navis farm. "You make such a handsome pair."

At Lina's hopeful look, Sarah merely sighed. Then, for the rest of the journey, she prayed and lost herself deep in thought.

She knew this predicament was of her own doing. She enjoyed the attention Richard paid her—she had even encouraged it. And, finally, Sarah concluded that she did love Richard, something which greatly surprised her. Ever since she was a young girl, she had fancied herself married to someone like Captain Sinclair, but more so since she'd met her sister-in-law, Valerie. Love, however, hadn't been a part of that fantasy. Sarah had merely assumed that she'd grow to love whomever she married. But affluence, ambition, a darkly handsome face, and mysterious disposition...those were the traits Sarah had longed for in a man. And, in her dreams, that man looked very much like Captain Sinclair.

Sarah shifted uncomfortably now as she admitted the truth to herself. All summer long she had avoided it, but here it was. The truth, like an incessant child, was crying and begging to be reckoned with, and Sarah could ignore it no longer.

She was drawn to the captain. Yes, it was true. And he tempted her to the point where she violated her conscience...like when they had waltzed together alone in the ballroom. But Sarah was sometimes uneasy around the captain as well. He was too...too familiar with her. Sarah was not accustomed to that sort of behavior. The captain thought nothing of taking her hand in his. Or smiling into her eyes. Or holding her close as they danced that one day. . .

Sarah squirmed. Her conscience still pricked her about that incident. She had been raised quite differently in her conservative Christian home. However, the captain was not a Christian, nor did he even seem interested in the Savior. No, he was not the man for her; Sarah was suddenly certain about at least that much! She'd been foolish, she realized, to even consider him, even if only in her dreams.

On the other hand, Richard loved the Lord and lived for him. And Richard was handsome, though he was more of a rascal than "mysterious." As for affluent and ambitious, those words did not describe him, at least not in the monetary sense. Hard-working and determined were better adjectives. And, except for one stolen kiss—which had been more given than stolen—Richard was a fine gentleman. However, "farmer" said it all!

Lord, help! Sarah silently pleaded as Tim pulled into the Navises' circle drive. *Help me discern my future. Help me know what I should do about Richard.*

Then, suddenly, the Lord gave her heart a reply, right from the Book of Psalms: "Be of good courage, and he shall strengthen your heart." All Sarah could do was give thanks in return. Her Savior was the One who truly understood her. He knew her heart, as fickle as it was. Then Sarah sighed as the peace of God which passes all understanding filled her soul. Why should she be so concerned when God was in control?

❧

Richard, too, had been praying on the way back to the farm, Fervently, in fact. He prayed that he'd be able to keep his promise to Sarah and that something would be settled between them. The only problem was, Richard had no idea what that "something" might be.

After a light lunch was served and after little Rachel was put down for her nap, he finally got a chance to speak with Sarah privately. Then they sat together on the steps of the wide, cement front porch which ran the entire width of the house. It was covered by an overhanging roof, shaded and very cool. Meanwhile, Gabriel, Michael, and Libby splashed happily in the pond near the apple orchard; somewhere in the fields beyond the cattle were lowing.

"Sarah, I think—"

"No, Richard, let me begin. May I?"

Surprised by her question, he nodded, although not without a twinge of trepidation. Sarah had been thoughtful for the last hour and a half. Would what she have to say break his heart forever?

"You're quite a stinker, Richard," she began.

He grinned. "Such flattery, Sarah. Really!"

She shook her head at him. "I realized on the way here today that I have to be honest with myself. . .and with you." She cleared her throat. "I need to tell you that. . .that you have succeeded in. . ." She paused, looking Richard square in the eyes. "Well, I do love you. Truly, I do."

He narrowed his gaze. "Don't tease me, Sarah. Not like that."

"I'm not teasing!"

"Sarah, I'm about to break into a few bars of the 'Hallelujah Chorus,' here! Don't tease me!"

She lifted an impish brow. "Will you be singing soprano or alto?"

"Whichever you'd prefer," he said with a wide grin. "I think I could do just about anything right now."

Sarah laughed as Richard, in falsetto, sang a poor rendition of Handel's beloved piece.

"Stop!" she finally cried. "Stop, please! The music teacher in me beseeches you!"

But she was giggling so hard that the children came running from the pond to see what all the ruckus was about.

"I'm afraid it's heat stroke," she told the children. "Perhaps we'll have to throw Mr. Navis in the pond to clear his head."

"Yes, let's do it!" they cried in unison.

"Oh, now, Miss Sarah is only joking," Richard told the children as he rose from the steps. Then he descended several of them. "But, tell you what: I'll come over in a few minutes and. . .well, maybe I'll let you throw me in after all. This heat is oppressive!"

With a cheer, the children went running back to the pond.

"If I had extra clothes," Sarah said, "I'd let them throw me in the pond, too."

"Extra clothes could easily be arranged," Richard replied with a twinkle in his eye. "Now tell me again that you love me."

"I don't know," Sarah replied, feigning a hesitant tone. "Look what happened the last time I did that!"

Richard grew suddenly serious. "Will you marry me, Sarah?"

"Oh, Richard, I haven't gotten that far yet," she said earnestly. "Will you give me some time? I mean, this farm. . .well, a girl has dreams, you know. I made myself a vow that I would work my way up the social ladder and never settle for the simple country life. But here you are, suddenly the man I love, asking me to do exactly that. In essence, Richard, you're asking me to give up my aspirations!"

For several long moments, Richard considered her words carefully. Then, finally, he nodded. "All right. Fair enough. I'll give you all the time you need. I'll love you forever, Sarah, so I guess I can wait until you change your mind about being a socialite." He grinned mischievously.

"Oh, why do I feel doomed?" Sarah asked dramatically, throwing her arms in the air.

Richard just laughed. "Here," he said, "give me your hand."

"Why?"

"Give me your hand."

Sarah complied and Richard pulled her to her feet. One good yank and she was in his arms. But now, as he carried her toward the pond, Sarah grew wise to his intentions.

"Don't you dare, Richard Navis!"

He just kept walking and grinning.

"Richard, I mean it! Don't you dare!"

Sarah struggled, but he held on fast.

"Stop, Richard!" she pleaded as they neared the pond. "I can't get wet. I'm supposed to be a lady!"

"Aw, Sarah, I won't tell."

"Richard!"

He chuckled and, heaving her upward, tossed her into the deepest part of the pond—about two feet deep. With a cry of indignation and a sound splash, Sarah hit the water, petticoats, stockings, leather ankle boots with their spool heels, and all. The children squealed with delight.

"Richard Navis, I can't believe you did that!" Sarah cried. She looked from the laughing children to Richard's grinning face, and she shook her wet head at the lot of them. Then she sighed, "Oh, this feels wonderful!"

Grabbing Michael's leg, Sarah pulled the boy down and under the cool water. He came up surprised, but laughing all the while.

Next she went after Libby, who did a grand imitation of Sarah's "Don't you dare! Don't you dare!" Warnings ignored, Libby too got dunked, but came up giggling hysterically.

Then Richard and Gabriel got into it, and both went under, laughing and splashing.

Suddenly Lina appeared and shook her head at them. "I won't even ask who instigated this nonsense," she said, looking pointedly at Richard who was lounging at one end of the pond.

From the other end, Sarah called, "Come on in, the water's fine."

A sudden gleam flashed in Richard's eyes and he sprang from the pond.

"Oh, no you don't!" Lina cried, and she took off running.

Richard chased his cousin into the orchard and everyone in the pond could hear Lina screaming. This brought Tim to the rescue.

"What in the world. . . !" he exclaimed, looking horrified.

Richard carried Lina back, kicking and pleading, but try as she might, she couldn't escape. Poor Tim looked too stunned to be of any help, so Lina also ended up in the pond.

"This does feel rather good, doesn't it?"

Sarah nodded.

Then suddenly Tim jumped in on his own accord, causing a gigantic splash, and everyone laughed until their sides ached.

Finally Marty Navis wheeled his chair onto the lawn. He laughed at the sight, then called, "I came to tell you there's a storm approaching. Look to the west!"

At once, everyone turned to stare at the great, ominous, black clouds and, in the sudden hush, they heard the distant rumbling of thunder.

"I'd best tend to the animals," Richard said.

"I'll help you, brother," Tim replied.

"I'll get the children into dry clothes," Sarah said, taking Libby's hand.

Lina nodded and followed Sarah. The afternoon's fun in the pond was suddenly over.

fifteen

The dark clouds drew closer and the thunder louder. But upstairs, safe inside the Navises' home, Sarah helped Libby into dry clothes while Lina tended to Rachel who had just awakened from her nap. Each little girl wore her cotton chemise from this morning, which could properly suffice as a nightshirt for now. Gabriel and Michael, however, had to change into their good church clothes. Then for Sarah, Lina found a simple calico dress and petticoat, minus the crinoline.

"I hope this will do," Lina said. "I left these items here last year, if I remember correctly. But my mother and I usually keep some clothes here, in case of emergencies. And our entire family comes and spends days at a time on the farm," she explained. "So we're always forgetting and leaving things behind."

Sarah gladly accepted the dress and under-things. They weren't very stylish, but they were dry. Then Lina found dry garments for herself. Sarah noticed that the clothes Lina and her mother had left at the farm were all as simple as the calico dress Sarah was borrowing. Of course they had no need for fancy attire on a farm. Modest and practical, that was what a woman's clothes needed to be on the farm. Sarah knew that from her growing up years in rural Missouri.

"Do you and your family come often?" Sarah asked.

"Twice a year," Lina replied. Then she grinned broadly. "Just think. . .after you marry Richard, you and I will be related. And Tim and I can come stay with you and Richard on holidays!"

Sarah rolled her eyes at Lina's presumption.

Suddenly the room grew dark as night and a strong gust of wind blew through the tree tops outside the open bedroom window.

"I'm scared!" cried Libby.

"Me too!" Rachel said in her baby voice. "I don't yike the thunder!"

"Oh, don't worry," Sarah told them, closing the window as Lina lit the lamp. "Jesus will take care of us."

Just then, Bea called up the stairs to them. "Come down quickly, girls. Marty thinks it's a twister coming!"

Lina extinguished the lamp she'd just lit, and then she and Sarah each grabbed a little girl. They hurried down the stairs where they met Gabriel, Michael, Tim, and the Navis family. Then they all took cover in the summer kitchen under the house. Marty went first in his wheel chair, accepting help from Richard and Tim. Then two oil lamps were lit, and Richard found some old barrels which served as seats for the men while the ladies took the chairs around the large, square work table.

"Let's play some chess," Marty suggested with a challenging grin.

"Yes, let's!" cried Gabriel and Michael.

The rain pelted the cellar door as the wind raged. And then it was over, just as fast as it had come, one of those wild, summer storms. Richard and Tim lifted the cellar door, and they chuckled, for the sun was beginning to shine again. The temperature was twenty degrees cooler than it had been earlier, and now the angry dark clouds were blowing eastward, over the lake—all very typical of Wisconsin summer storms.

Marty Navis was carried upstairs, after which Richard, Tim, Gabriel, and Michael walked around the property, looking for damage. They came back nearly an hour later, reporting a few downed trees. But that was all.

"And it looks as though the Staffords' property is fine, too," Richard announced as they all sat down to supper. Now that the oppressive heat was gone, appetites had returned.

Bea smiled as she served up the hastily prepared meal of fried eggs, ham, and sliced homemade bread.

When supper was finished, Marty requested his Bible and read from Isaiah chapter twenty-five: " 'For thou hast been a strength to the poor, a strength to the needy in his distress, a refuge from the storm, a shadow from the heat, when the blast of the terrible ones is as a storm against the wall. . . .' " He looked around the table. "Let's bow our heads and give God thanks for protecting us today."

Sarah lowered her chin as a hush fell over the group. Just then Libby tugged on her skirt.

"Miss Sarah," she whispered, loud enough for all to hear, "Jesus really did keep us safe, didn't He?"

Sarah smiled and nodded. Then she closed her eyes to give thanks.

"Miss Sarah," Libby's voice came again, "can I pray, too? Will you show me?"

After a moment's pause, Sarah realized that Libby was ready to accept Jesus into her heart! Sarah looked at Richard, who winked and nodded encouragingly.

"Come, Libby," Sarah whispered back. Then she took the child's hand. "Let's go pray together."

"Can I come, too?" Michael asked, and Marty Navis never even got started with his prayer of thanksgiving.

"Me, too," Gabriel asked as well.

Richard stood and grinned broadly. "Come on. Let's all of us go pray together."

Bea held Rachel on her lap while Sarah and Richard led the other children into a quiet spot in the front room.

"Before we pray," Richard began, "I want to tell you about four things that God wants you to know. First of all, He wants you to know that you're a sinner. Do you know what sin is?"

The children nodded, but Libby was the one who replied, "Sin is when you do something wrong. Like tell a fib."

"That's right," Richard said. "The Bible says in Romans 3:23, 'For all have sinned, and come short of the glory of God.' You

see, I'm a sinner and Sarah is a sinner, too. The only difference
is, Sarah and I have been forgiven of our sins by God. But if
you aren't forgiven by God, then, like the Bible says, 'The wages
of sin is death.' The Bible also says, 'And whosoever was not
found written in the book of life was cast into the lake of fire.' "
Richard looked at each child. "That's a description of hell—the
lake of fire. See, that's the second thing God wants you to know:
Sinners who aren't forgiven can't go to heaven."

"Well, I want to go to heaven!" Michael declared. His siblings nodded in agreement.

Richard smiled. "Good. Then here's the third thing God wants
you to know: Jesus Christ died for all sinners. In the Bible it says,
'For God so loved the world, that he gave his only begotten
Son, that whosoever believeth in him should not perish, but
have everlasting life.' You see, Jesus is God and He was perfect.
He never sinned, so He was our substitute."

Richard frowned, seeing the children's puzzled faces. *How can
I explain it better?* he wondered.

Then Sarah said, "Jesus got the spanking that you should have
gotten when you sinned. Jesus took your punishment. . .to save
you."

"Oh," said the children, nodding in understanding now.

Richard sent a look of gratitude Sarah's way, and she smiled.

"All right, now here's the fourth thing God wants you to know,"
Richard continued. "Anyone can be saved. The Bible says, 'If thou
shalt confess with thy mouth the Lord Jesus, and shalt believe in
thine heart that God hath raised him from the dead, thou shalt
be saved.' " Richard looked at each of the children. "Jesus died
on the cross, but He didn't stay dead. God raised Him up again—
brought Him back to life. And that's what God will do for you,
too, if you believe what I just told you." Richard smiled gently.
"Do you believe what the Bible says about Jesus?"

"Yes," they said in unison.

Then Gabriel added. "We get teached that in Sunday school."

"Taught," Sarah corrected him.

He nodded.

"Well, if you believe what the Bible says about sin and about what Jesus did to take away your sin," Richard told the children now, "then you can pray and ask God to forgive you and ask Jesus into your heart where He'll live forever. Do you want to do that?"

The Sinclair children each nodded.

Sarah lowered her head and Libby followed. Then the boys did the same, and Richard instructed all the children to repeat after him. . .

"Dear God, I know I am a sinner and deserve to go to hell. But I am truly sorry for my sins and I ask Your forgiveness. I know Jesus died to save me with His shed blood and I ask for Him to come into my heart. I here and now accept Your free gift of salvation through Jesus Christ, Your Son. Amen."

"Amen!" Sarah said, looking up and smiling brightly.

"Amen!" Gabriel and Michael said, too.

Then Libby added her own, "Amen!"

❧

Later that night Tim, Lina, Sarah, and the children at last rolled out of the Navises' circle drive. The air was cool and crisp, and the sky was clear; the stars were shining above like sprinklings of silver.

Sarah was still awed that Gabriel and Michael and Libby had seen their need for the Savior. Libby had even said later that she "felt happier" which made Sarah want to rejoice all the more. Then she was reminded that the angels in heaven were rejoicing tonight, too. Looking heavenward, Sarah breathed deeply and smiled.

"It seems you and Richard have gotten things squared away," Lina remarked.

Sarah continued to smile. "Yes, I suppose we have."

"And?"

"And what?"

"A wedding date?"

On the other side of Lina, Tim's chuckle could be heard.

"What's so funny?" Lina demanded.

"You, my sweet," he replied. "You're quite the little match-maker."

Lina swatted Tim's arm playfully while Sarah laughed. But suddenly they quieted, and Sarah knew an answer was expected, all joking aside.

She cleared her throat. "Well, uh, no wedding date. Not yet."

"Oh, what a shame." Lina sounded disappointed.

"Well, marriage is a big step." Sarah felt a need to explain herself. "One has to be certain. And. . .well. . .living on a farm is not what I had planned for my life. I've told you this before, and I mean no personal offense to the Navis family in the least. It's just that I. . .well. . .I had always thought I'd live in a house like Captain Sinclair's house. . ."

"And marry a man like the captain, too, I presume," said Tim. "He's handsome and rich, and I wouldn't doubt that he turns many a woman's head with his velveteen words."

"I'm sure he does," Sarah replied curtly, "however, the captain is not a believer and. . .no, I have no desire to marry him."

"Well, perhaps not him, *personally*," Tim said, "but a man *like* him."

Sarah couldn't deny the comment. Yes, it was true; she had imagined herself married to a man *like* Captain Sinclair. She was fascinated with him and his lifestyle, his magnificent home, and his rich, important friends.

"I can't help but think of what the Bible says about men like the captain," Tim was saying. Then he quoted Matthew 16:26: " 'For what is a man profited, if he shall gain the whole world, and lose his own soul?' "

"Nothing," Sarah replied. "He is profited nothing except an eternity in hell."

"My thoughts exactly," Tim said. "And all the captain's money will do him little good on judgment day."

Sarah sighed impatiently. "What is your point, Tim? What are you saying?"

"I'm saying that you ought to take your eyes off the captain and start focusing on what's really important here. Richard is a good, honest man who loves the Lord. . .and who loves you, too, Sarah McCabe!"

She gasped indignantly and set her chin stubbornly. *The nerve of that man to talk to me in such a way!* she fumed.

Lina patted Sarah's hand reassuringly, but Sarah had to force herself not to pull away.

Long and uncomfortable minutes passed; then, as the wagon moved eastward toward the city, Sarah turned and checked on the children. She hoped they hadn't overheard that last discussion.

"Are they sleeping?" Lina asked.

"Yes. And baby Rachel has snuggled right up against Gabriel . . .just like I used to snuggle against my big brothers." Sarah smiled at the memory.

"Well, I never had any big brothers, or any siblings," Lina said. "I'm an only child, just like Richard, although he's as close to me as any brother could be."

Another long moment of silence passed.

"Richard says your brothers are missionaries," Tim said, his voice conciliatory. "Is that true?"

Sarah had to swallow her previous annoyance at him in order to answer civilly: "Yes, that's true. But only two brothers are missionaries. The other is a photographer in St. Louis."

"And the missionaries. . .are they married?" Tim asked.

"Not yet," Sarah replied. Then she had to smile, thinking of Jacob and Luke. "Both are such rascals! Serious Christians, but rascals all the same. It'll take two special women to tame them, I'm afraid."

Lina giggled. "That's what I always said about Richard, isn't it, Tim?"

"Yes, indeed." Tim paused. "Well, I'll certainly pray, Sarah, that when your brothers do find women to love, they won't be scorned merely because they're missionaries. I mean, there's not much prestige in missionary work, but there sure is an awful lot of sacrifice involved."

"And persecution," Lina added. "Missionaries have been known to be burned at the stake, pierced with arrows, buried alive. . . stoned to death, like Stephen was in the Book of Acts."

"Quite true, Lina," Tim said. "And to be scorned by the woman you love would hurt terribly—another kind of torture, I'd say!"

Tim's words struck Sarah like a slap and suddenly she saw things very differently. She would hate if a woman refused either of her brothers simply because he was doing what God willed. She would think that kind of woman was unworthy of her brother. Furthermore, she would think of that woman as prideful and haughty.

And yet, wasn't that exactly the way she was behaving toward Richard?

Fat tears slid down Sarah's cheeks and she felt like she'd been snapped in two. She suddenly realized, much to her horror, that she had been acting wickedly by allowing herself to be tempted by the captain and his influence, his wealth, and all his beautiful things. How ashamed of their youngest daughter her parents would be, Sarah decided, if they could see how she had tossed her careful upbringing aside.

Forgive me, Lord, she prayed silently. *Forgive me for not seeking Your will in all of this but, instead, seeking my own. Help me now to right any wrongs that I've done. . .*

Then, without a word, Lina put a consoling arm around her as Tim passed down his handkerchief, and Sarah accepted both gestures of kindness graciously.

sixteen

Sarah climbed down from the wagon, with Tim's help, and then both he and Lina helped her carry the children upstairs to bed. After seeing Tim and Lina on their way, Sarah retired to her bedroom and wrote to her parents.

Dear Mother and Father:

I need to confess to you, since I have already confessed my sin to God, that I have behaved badly toward Richard. He's a wonderful young man and, Pa, you will like him. I believe I do love him and I told him so today. I had been hesitant to make any sort of commitment because I didn't want to live on a farm. I thought I was too good for farm life. You see, Richard has chosen farming instead of bookkeeping—but I'm sure he told you all that in his last letter.

Tonight I realized that I have been harboring a haughty spirit and, as the Bible warns, a haughty spirit goes before a fall—I believe mine came tonight.

What I also need for you to know is that I am willing to marry Richard. . .even if he has chosen farming as a way of life. I believe it is God's will for my life; He has shown me many things this summer. Of course, you will have to approve before I can accept Richard's proposal of marriage; however, he has asked. Several times, in fact. Each time I refused him simply and solely

> *because he has chosen to be a farmer.*
>   *So now, seeing as I am forgiven by God, I*
> *need to ask Richard's forgiveness as well, but I*
> *know he will forgive me because he loves me. . .*

Sarah paused to collect her thoughts. Then she continued writing, telling her parents about today's storm and of Gabriel, Michael, and Libby's salvation decisions. Sarah wrote freely, describing the Navises' farm, its out-buildings, the animals, the gardens, the orchard and. . .the pond.

> *And he threw me in! Why, my fine leather*
> *boots will squish and squash for weeks when I*
> *walk. That prank was something Luke would*
> *enjoy!*

Then Sarah wrote about how Marty Navis had built the house in 1851. She described how unusual it was, not at all a typical farmhouse. Sarah had never relayed the story to her parents, but now, for some reason, she felt compelled to tell them everything about Richard and his family.

Finally, with her letter finished and ready to be posted, Sarah left her bedroom to check on the happenings within the household. It was after nine o'clock and Gretchen was home, but apparently the captain was not.

"I'm going up to the vidow's valk, Irish," Gretchen said; however, her tone held no note of malice, just fear and weariness.

"May I come?" Sarah ventured to ask, wondering what was bothering Gretchen.

"You may."

Sarah had never been up on the widow's walk before, though she knew the captain enjoyed being up there. He had a large telescope with which one could look out over Lake Michigan, and Gabriel had once told Sarah that he'd been given a chance to look through it on several occasions.

"He is out there somewhere," Gretchen murmured now,

looking out over the vast body of water.

"Who is?" Sarah asked.

"Captain Sinclair." Gretchen heaved a great sigh. "This evening, about seven o'clock, a man named Mr. Craine delivered a message. It said that the captain's small schooner, *The Adventuress*, was discovered in pieces after today's storm. No bodies have been recovered yet, but all on board are presumed dead."

"No!" Sarah cried as fingers of horror ran up her spine. The captain? Dead? Aurora? It couldn't be true!

"It could be months before the bodies are recovered," Gretchen said, shaking her head sadly. "It's happened before."

"Don't say that!" Sarah cried again. "They could be alive. Perhaps they made it safely to shore and we just don't know it yet!"

Gretchen didn't reply, and a long moment passed between the two women who stood gazing out over the murderous waves of Lake Michigan.

"I had to give Mr. Craine the names of those aboard *The Adventuress*, and I vasn't sure. . ."

Sarah thought a moment. "Aurora."

"Yes."

"And the captain, of course. And Mrs. Kingsley."

"Yes, yes. . ."

"And Mr.—oh, what was his name again?"

"St. Martin."

"That's right."

"Any others?" Gretchen asked.

"Not that I know of."

Then it hit Sarah—and the truth, like a thunderbolt, shook her to the very core of her being. *If I had given in to my temptation,* she thought, *and gone sailing with the captain today. . .I would have been. . .and the children. . .we would be among those presumed dead!*

Sarah immediately thanked God for His Holy Spirit which had prompted her to obey Him.

Another long moment passed in silence and Sarah felt more

and more sick inside. Heartsick.

"It's like a bad dream," she murmured. "I wish this wasn't happening. I mean, what of the children? I suppose we shouldn't tell them anything until we hear some definite news."

"Yes, I suppose. . ." Gretchen was silent for a while and then finally she said, "I have a feeling it's all over, Irish. The captain is dead and my life's vork has drowned in that lake vith him." She shook her head. "Life can be so unkind!"

Then, before Sarah had a chance to reply, Gretchen turned and went quickly into the house.

&

The night passed fretfully for Sarah. She spent much of it praying as hard as she could that the captain, his mother, and their friends had somehow survived the storm.

But such seemed not to be God's will. Richard arrived the next morning with the bad news.

"Two bodies have been recovered," he told Sarah and Gretchen. "I've been asked, as the captain's steward, to go and identify them right now." He sighed, raking a troubled hand through his blond hair. "This is not something I relish doing!"

"Would it help if I went along?" Sarah asked. She really didn't want to go, but she would do it for Richard.

However, he shook his head. "It's not a sight any woman should have to see, I think. You and Gretchen stay here. Try not to upset yourselves overmuch. I'll be back in a couple of hours."

As Richard left, Sarah wished she could tell him of her decision last night. She was willing to marry him, farm and all. Right now he seemed so gallant and brave. But this other business was more important now; she would have to wait to talk to him about her decision.

"You could do a lot vorse than Richard Navis," Gretchen said tersely.

Sarah, however, was not offended in the least. "Actually, Mrs. Schlyterhaus," she replied, "I believe I couldn't do better than Richard Navis." And then Sarah forgot herself and ran up the front stairs to check on the children.

"The servant's stairvell, Irish!" Gretchen called. "Vill you ever learn?"

⁊⁊

Richard was back by suppertime, looking somber and distressed. As the children ate under the cook's supervision, he told Sarah and Gretchen that he had identified Elise Kingsley and Aurora.

Immediate tears stung Sarah's eyes as she sat down heavily on a chair in the main reception hall. *Aurora. Dead. The children's grandmother. Gone.*

"They're all dead, aren't they?" Gretchen asked, looking forlorn.

"I don't know," Richard replied. "We can only hope and pray. I would really hate to speculate at this point." He turned to Sarah. "Don't cry," he told her. Then, in an effort to comfort her, he took her hand.

"What should I tell the children?" she asked, wiping the tears from her cheeks.

"Tell them the truth," Richard told her. "As gently as you can, Sarah, you must tell them the truth."

"I vill help you, Irish," Gretchen announced with her usual stoic expression. "I love them, too, you know."

"I can help as well," Richard said. "Come, Sarah, let's tell them right now."

When the children had finished eating, they were taken for an evening stroll near the bluffs overlooking Lake Michigan. Richard did all the explaining while Sarah and Gretchen stood by for moral support. However, the children took the news very well. Solemnly, with only a few tears.

They're in shock, the poor dears, Sarah thought because of the little emotion each child showed. *They'll cry their eyes out later.*

"Is Aurora with Jesus?" Libby asked suddenly.

"She could be," Richard told the wide-eyed little girl. "And we can rejoice in the fact that Jesus is good and allows no one to die without hearing about the gift of eternal life through Him. I know Aurora heard the good news about Jesus—just like you did yesterday."

At that Libby smiled and the two older boys nodded. Sarah,

on the other hand, was grateful for Richard's tact regarding Aurora. She, personally, didn't think Aurora knew the Lord; however, only God could judge a person's soul.

A few more questions were thrown at Richard and then they all walked back to the house.

"It looks sad, too," Sarah observed.

"What?" Richard asked.

"The house. It looks sad, somehow. I can't really explain it."

"Maybe it's because you're looking at it through sad eyes, Sarah," Richard said. Then, as they climbed the stairs to the entranceway, he added, "I can stay for a while if you want me to."

Sarah nodded. "Yes, Richard, I want you to. Thank you."

He smiled, looking pleased in spite of all the tragedy surrounding them.

Inside the house, Sarah sent the children up the stairs, but hung back to speak with Richard privately for a moment. "I wrote to my parents last night," she said. "It was before I learned of the captain. . ."

"Well, that's nice," he replied, looking unsure as to why she was telling him this.

"The letter has to do with something I realized last night on the way home," Sarah explained. "The Lord used Tim and Lina to help me see things more clearly." She turned, producing the letter from where it sat on the hallway table. "I would like for you to read it."

Slowly, Richard took the proffered envelope and stared at it for several long moments. He looked like he was afraid to read it.

Sarah smiled. "I think the letter will encourage you, Richard; however, I must get the children to sleep now, so no hallelujahs, all right?"

He chuckled and opened the envelope. "All right."

Sarah walked through the hallway and passed the kitchen, using the servant's stairwell. For once, she actually remembered! Then, as she was just about to read Libby and Rachel a story, Richard entered the nursery.

"Excuse me, girls," he said to Libby and Rachel, "but I must borrow your governess for a moment."

Libby sighed. "All right, but just for a moment."

Sarah smiled, and Richard murmured that she was certainly a "bossy little thing." Then, taking Sarah's hand, he led her into the hallway.

"What is it?"

Richard grinned. "You have made me a very happy man. Do you really mean what you wrote in this letter?" He waved the envelope at her. "Or was it merely a surge of emotion?"

"I really mean every single word."

"And you're really going to post the letter and send it to your parents?"

"Well, of course I am! Why would I write all that and. . .and *not* post it?"

"Just making sure," Richard replied. He drew himself up, taking a large breath. "Sarah, I want to take you in my arms and kiss you until you swoon!"

She smiled impishly. "Well, that would be lovely, but Mrs. Schlyterhaus is somewhere about. She would most likely catch us."

Slowly, Richard nodded. "Well, then, I'll just have to control myself until I marry you."

Sarah's smile widened. "I shall wait for that day with bated breath."

Suddenly, from behind Richard, Gretchen cleared her throat. "The captain may not be here," she said stiffly, "but you are still on duty, Irish."

"Yes, I am. . .but only for another fifteen minutes." With that she gave Richard a meaningful look.

"I'll wait for you downstairs," he replied.

"But I want to stay around until I'm sure the children are sleeping."

"A good idea, Sarah."

And so, with a nod and a little smile, she turned and went back to attend to Libby and Rachel, her heart both heavy and glad, all at the same time.

seventeen

Several days passed and still no word came on Captain Sinclair; however, the body of Mr. St. Martin had surfaced and washed ashore. The news traveled through various social circles within the Milwaukee community until all of the captain's friends, acquaintances, and business associates knew that he was "missing at sea." Not a day went by when Sarah, the children, and Gretchen weren't bombarded with concerned and curious neighbors knocking at the front door and asking questions.

Then the day of Aurora's funeral arrived. Richard had arranged the entire affair, capable man that he was, and it was, for a funeral, very lovely. It was held at the Sinclair home, up in the ballroom, for it was the only room that could hold so many people. Gretchen had decorated the room in somber colors, and large vases of flowers graced every corner.

"I should hope that my wedding day is so grand," Lina whispered, surveying the room.

Sarah smiled. "If Aurora were here, I believe she would highly approve."

Lina nodded, and then she and Sarah took their places.

Each of the captain's children read selections from the Book of Psalms and then the pastor of the Navises' church got up and gave a brief message. He spoke on the importance of making decisions that affect eternity. Then he told of God's free gift of salvation and that, like every gift, one has to *decide* to accept it.

After the message, Sarah played the piano while Lina sang one of William Cowper's beloved hymns:

There is a fountain filled with blood
Drawn from Immanuel's veins;
And sinners, plunged beneath that flood,
Lose all their guilty stains.

The stirring melody proved to be another witness for Christ, for after the funeral many people were heard to ask, "What is the name of that beautiful song?" Even Gretchen, despite her rigid exterior, had wept openly while Lina sang. The children, too, were teary-eyed, causing several ladies and a few gentlemen to cast long, pitiful glances their way.

Then an afternoon luncheon was served, and Isabelle out-did herself in preparing the elegant food trays. After eating, friends and neighbors roamed the grounds. Men smoked cigars in the men's parlor, and ladies sipped iced tea in the ladies' parlor. Some people preferred to be outside or sit in the adjacent gazebo. Aurora's funeral, apparently, was a tremendous success socially. But more importantly, it was successful spiritually, for Richard said that several salvation decisions had been made.

By the end of the day, however, Sarah's nerves were frayed and, after the last guest left, she sat down on a chair in the kitchen and cried. Her sobs wracked her body, she cried so hard, and neither Lina nor her mother, Richard's Aunt Ruth, could comfort her. Even Richard had trouble consoling her.

Finally he made a decision: Sarah, Gretchen, and the children would live at the farm until further notice.

"Oh, I don't know if that's such a good idea, Richard," Sarah choked.

"I think it is," he replied. "Except I'm so busy right now, what with all the captain's business and this mess of him missing, that I can't look after you. But my mother can. . .and will. And, perhaps that's what you need right now. A little bit of mothering. Gretchen could use some reprieve also. What do you say?"

Unable to speak over her emotion, Sarah merely nodded.

"And I'll send a wire to your parents, letting them know what's happened."

Again, Sarah nodded. She was only too glad to let Richard handle this and oh! how thankful she was that she had him to depend on right now.

Marty and Bea Navis had attended Aurora's funeral also and they were all for the idea. That very evening, Sarah and the children were packed and ready to go. Gretchen, too, agreed to move to the farm, and Sarah watched as she carefully covered the captain's furniture with white bed sheets to protect them.

A haunting shiver, an oppressive chill, came over Sarah as she thought about the captain and all his beautiful things. His rich, important friends. His money. All he possessed could not save him from the angry waves of Lake Michigan.

" 'What is a man profited,' " she said aloud, quoting the Lord's own words, " 'if he shall gain the whole world, and lose his own soul?' "

Gretchen nodded solemnly. "The captain vas a good man. He vas not immoral, nor did he use profanity like some men do. But the captain's fault is that he vould not listen to the truth of the gospel."

" 'The care of this world,' " Sarah said, again quoting Jesus, " 'and the deceitfulness of riches, choke the word.' " She shook her head sadly. "And that's what happened, isn't it, Mrs. Schlyterhaus? The world got in the way of the captain's hearing the gospel."

"I vould say so." Gretchen grew bleary-eyed. "Come and help me, Irish!" she demanded, and Sarah sensed the gruffness was to cover her true emotions.

"Of course, I'll help," Sarah said, her throat constricting with a new onset of unshed tears. "What can I do?"

"Take an end and help me cover these things."

Together they covered the grand piano and the coffee tables. In the large dining room, they covered the table and chairs under one huge drape. In the kitchen, they helped Isabelle put everything away in cupboards while Aunt Ruth and Bea tended to the ice box. Outside, Richard, his father, and Uncle Jesse were with the children playing with a ball.

"Come, Irish," Gretchen said, after they'd finished in the kitchen. "Ve have more vork to do."

Sarah followed the housekeeper into the captain's study where she helped cover his desk, papers all askew, just the way the man had left them. Then Sarah and Gretchen covered the leather upholstered chairs. How tragic this was!

"You know, he may not be dead," Sarah stated at last.

"Oh, he's dead all right," Gretchen said. "Everyone else is dead."

Sarah merely shrugged. "Can't blame a girl for wishful thinking." She smiled. "I guess I believe in miracles."

Now it was Gretchen's turn to shrug.

Richard appeared outside the doorway, holding little Rachel in his arms. "The wagon is all packed and we're ready to roll when you are."

"I'm ready!" Sarah said at once. She turned and marched out of the captain's study, pausing in front of Richard. "If someone would have told me when I first came to this house that I'd one day be anxious to leave it, I would have laughed at the very idea!"

Richard gave her an understanding smile.

Then Sarah gave one last look around. "I am anxious to leave," she reiterated.

Richard nodded. "Well, then let's go!"

❧

Richard sent a telegraph message to Sarah's parents the following day and a response came the very next afternoon. Richard brought the message home with him that evening. It was Sarah's second day on the farm.

"Oh, no!" she exclaimed. "Luke is coming to fetch me and I'm not to return to Chicago on September first!"

Richard frowned. "Your parents are angry, then, Sarah?"

"I don't know."

The young couple considered each other speculatively from where they stood in the front yard beneath the colorful evening sky. Splashes of orange and gray were painted on the horizon, but neither Sarah nor Richard could appreciate the scenery at the moment.

"Sarah, honestly, I sent the best, most informative wire I could afford," Richard told her.

"I'm sure you did," Sarah replied. "It's not your fault. And thank you again for sending it."

He paused, but only momentarily. "Your teaching position, Sarah. . .are you sorry to lose it?"

She smiled. "Not at all. In fact, I had already given it up in my heart when I decided I'd like to marry you."

Now Richard smiled and a love-light shone from the depths of his eyes. Nevertheless, Sarah decided to tease him.

"I imagine that my parents got my last letter and now Luke is coming to check you out like a prize thoroughbred."

"I guess I'm flattered," Richard replied, feigning a look of uncertainty. Then he grinned. "Will your brother examine my teeth as well?"

"No, but you had better memorize the entire Bible!"

She said it in jest, but then suddenly sat down heavily on the porch step. Her nerves were as taut as the clothesline hanging out back, and tears pooled in her eyes from the mounting tension. First the captain, who was probably drowned, then Aurora's funeral, moving to the farm, not to mention trying to be strong for the children's sakes. And now Luke, coming to fetch her and take her home. . .

"What's wrong, Sarah?" Richard asked gently.

She sniffed. "Everything. And you may change your mind about marrying me once you meet my brother, Luke."

Richard laughed. "I doubt it."

"I hope you won't," Sarah said.

"I won't." Richard took her hand. "I love you, Sarah. That's for always and forever. And let's not forget that God is in control. 'The king's heart is in the hand of the Lord, as the rivers of water: he turneth it whithersoever he will.'"

Sarah recognized the passage at once and it brought a smile to her lips. "Proverbs 21:1."

"That's right. And it means that God is the ultimate authority. Would you agree?"

"Yes." And then a surge of peace suddenly replaced the anxiety in Sarah's heart.

Just then Bea appeared at the front doorway. "I've prepared a bath for you, Sarah," she said. "I know it's only Tuesday, and bath day is Saturday around here, but I had a notion that it might calm your nerves."

Sarah's spirits soared. "Oh, Mrs. Navis!" she cried gratefully. "A bath will fix everything!" She turned to Richard. "Will you excuse me, please?"

He chuckled. "Of course."

Getting up from the step, Sarah followed Bea through the house and down to the summer kitchen where a curtain hung around the tub to ensure privacy.

"Thank you," Sarah said, giving Bea a hug. "How did you know I needed this?"

"Oh, well," the older woman replied, looking embarrassed, "a good soaking does wonders for my disposition and somehow I just knew it would do wonders for yours, too."

Bea handed Sarah a clean towel. It was stiff, but smelled of fresh air and sunshine, having been hung out on the line to dry.

"Now you just take your time, Sarah dear," Bea instructed her, heading for the door now. "Rest in that tub a good while and soon you'll feel just as good as new!"

"Yes, ma'am," Sarah replied. Then, before undressing, she dipped her fingers in the water. "Perfect," she murmured. "Simply perfect!"

After more than a week on the Navises' farm, and some more extra doses of tender loving care from Bea, Sarah felt rested and regained her composure. The stressful weight she'd been carrying grew lighter as she continually gave it over to the Lord in prayer.

The children, too, settled into a comfortable routine and began to push the tragedy concerning their father aside; however, they still had many questions which Sarah and the Navises did their best to answer. Mostly, though, they kept the children busy and happy. They were up early in the mornings and helped milk the cows and feed the pigs and chickens. They each chose a kitten for their very own. Gabriel named his "Killer," while Libby called hers "Fluffy." Michael's kitty was "Jimmie," and Rachel simply called hers, "Kiddykiddy."

Sarah, too, kept busy, and she began to meet Bethany in the garden around the same time each day. They talked amicably as they picked green beans, strawberries, and peas—Bethany picking on her side of the property line. The boys had been assigned to the cornfield while the little girls napped in the afternoons, and Gretchen stayed busy in the summer kitchen, helping Bea can the vegetables for the winter months.

On this particular day, Bethany came out to the garden and picked and chatted as always. But then she grew quiet and suddenly Sarah noticed that she was crying.

"Beth, what is it?" Sarah asked, dropping her basket of peas. She walked the short distance through the rows of vegetables to where Bethany stood. "Tell me, what's wrong?"

"Oh, it's Lionel," she finally confessed. "He's broken our engagement."

Sarah put a compassionate arm around her. "I'm sorry to hear that, Beth."

"He said he doesn't love me," she choked.

"What a horrible thing to say!" Sarah locked arms with Bethany. "I have an idea. Why don't you come on over for some lemonade.

Mrs. Navis made a pitcher this morning. It's so tart, it'll make you pucker, but it sure tastes good on a hot day."

Bethany nodded her acquiescence, and Sarah couldn't help thinking that, as Bea Navis had shown her love and compassion, her turn had come to show the same toward Bethany.

They walked through the garden to the house and, once inside the kitchen, Sarah said, "Sit down, there at the table, Beth, and rest. We'll talk this whole thing out and you'll feel better."

"There is nothing to discuss, Sarah!" Bethany declared. "I am never giving my heart to another man as long as I live and that's that!"

"Now, now, don't be hasty."

"Lionel is the second man to say he doesn't love me." She gave Sarah an almost guilty look. "Richard was the first."

Sarah felt a twinge of remorse for her, but not pity since she had had an inkling that Lionel was the wrong man for Bethany from the start.

"I remember my father telling my older sister Leah that she couldn't give her heart to any man until she gave it to Jesus first," Sarah told Bethany. "And, from watching my sister, I learned that important lesson without having to experience the heartache she did." Sarah sipped her lemonade. "So, while I can't relate to your feelings in that respect, Beth, I do know that it's far better for you to learn now that Lionel isn't the man whom God has chosen for you than to be locked in an unhappy marriage."

Bethany nodded. "I suppose you're right." She wiped away an errant tear. "But it still hurts."

"I'm sure it does. Here, let me give you a hug." She did, and then Sarah smiled impishly. "Would you like a kitten, too? That did wonders for the children."

Bethany rolled her eyes and shook her light brown head. Freckles were splattered across her nose from the summer sunshine. "We have dozens of kittens on our farm, Sarah McCabe. I think my mother would tan my hide if I came home with another one!"

Sarah laughed and even Bethany managed a smile. But just a little one.

eighteen

The second week of September, Luke McCabe got off the train at Union Depot in downtown Milwaukee. Richard recognized him at once from Sarah's description. He was tall, blond, and broad-shouldered, and he wore a dark suit which contrasted with his light features and bright blue eyes. In one hand, he carried a wide-brimmed hat; he held his baggage in the other.

"Pastor McCabe," Richard called.

"Yes?" He looked surprised. Then he smiled and set down his bags. "You must be Mr. Navis."

Richard nodded. "Please call me Richard."

"Very well." Luke shook his hand.

"Here, let me help you with your things," Richard said.

Leaving the train station, the two men climbed into one of the captain's carriages. Under the circumstances, Richard didn't think the captain would mind. His estate would be completely liquidated at the end of the month, both the house and the business would be sold. Richard was handling it all, with the help, of course, of Captain Sinclair's attorneys. For all his dislike of figures and calculations, Richard seemed to be doing just that lately. . .until he got home in the evenings. Then the children came running from the yard to greet him with sweet Sarah not far behind. Her welcoming smile was the highlight of Richard's day!

"How is Sarah?" her brother now asked.

"She's well," Richard replied. "This whole thing with the captain shook her badly, but I think she is recovering."

"Good. The folks at home have been quite concerned. Me included. The wire you sent was most disturbing."

"I understand. But there wasn't any good way of conveying the sort of news I had to send your family."

"I suppose that's true enough."

They rode a ways in silence, leaving the city behind them. Finally, Luke spoke again.

"So you want to marry Sarah, huh?"

"That's right." Richard smiled.

"From her last letter, I gather that she wants to marry you, too."

"Yes, sir. And it's a direct answer to prayer. . .for me."

Luke lifted the corners of his mouth in an amused grin. "Well, I need to tell you that I'm planning to talk my baby sister into coming out West with me. We need a school teacher in a mighty bad way."

Richard didn't even flinch at the challenge. Sarah had warned him, saying Luke would try to dissuade him. "But don't let him talk you out of marrying me," she had said with a lovely pout. Recalling that conversation now, Richard grinned.

"You're not worried?" Luke asked.

"No, sir," Richard replied.

"Hmmm. . ."

And that, for the time being, was the end of that.

"So, tell me about yourself, Richard."

He did, for the rest of the ride home. He talked of his parents, his upbringing, his education, his position with the captain, and, finally, his decision to buy his father's farm and work the fields. Then he told Luke of this summer's events with Sarah, how they had met, how he had come to love her.

"Sarah is very easy to love," Luke stated candidly. "Half the men in our small hometown, just outside of St. Louis, were in love with her at one time or another. The other half are relatives."

Richard chuckled. "Yes, Sarah has told me."

"She prepared you, huh?"

"That's it."

Richard pulled into the circle drive of his family's home. The children came running around the house, but when they saw the stranger, they paused.

"This is Pastor McCabe," Richard called to them. "He's Miss Sarah's brother. No need to be afraid. Come say hello."

Gabriel and Michael came forward immediately to shake hands, but Libby hung back, and Rachel ran away.

Then Sarah appeared. "Luke!" she cried with a huge smile.

"Hey, there, baby sister," he returned, scooping her up in his arms and then twirling her around once. He set a kiss upon her forehead. "Well, you look no worse for wear."

Richard chuckled softly as he unloaded the buggy.

"In fact," Luke was saying, "you're much too pretty to take out West. Why, I'd be challenged daily since those cowboys would be falling all over themselves just looking at you!"

Sarah pulled back. "Out West!" She glanced at Richard with a light of horror in her eyes.

Meeting her gaze, he merely sent her a confident wink.

Last night they had talked about this, about Luke's arrival. Richard's mother encouraged the young couple greatly by reminding them that if God intended them to marry, they would. With that wise piece of advice, she had quoted Philippians 4:6.

"We'll talk later, baby sister," Luke was telling Sarah now. "I've got an adventure in mind for you, and I know you're not one to turn down an adventure."

"You may be surprised at my reaction, Luke," she replied with a sweet smile. "You may be very surprised. . ."

෴

After a hearty supper of roast beef, mashed potatoes, fresh spinach, and corn on the cob, Richard showed Luke to his room. It was wide and comfortable and right across the hall from Sarah's room. The children slept in a bedroom at the end of the hallway, (the boys having had to forfeit their room for Luke's sake), and Mr. and Mrs. Navis slept in their own bedroom on the first floor. Gretchen slept in the adjacent parlor which had been made over into a bedroom to accommodate her, and Richard slept out in the barn. The latter had troubled Luke a bit, as he imagined the poor boy in the hayloft. But then Richard showed him around the property and, when they went into the barn, Luke was surprised to find a bunkhouse built into the side of it.

"In the past," Richard explained, "we've had to hire planters and pickers. We let them bunk in here. But, since Sarah, Gretchen, and the children moved in, I've been sleeping out here."

"Quite appropriate," Luke remarked. "And I thank you kindly for taking such good care of my sister."

Richard smiled. "It has been entirely my privilege."

"Yes, so I've gathered." Luke was now smiling as well.

They left the barn and walked back to the house. In the living room, Luke sat down and observed some of the goings-on. Sarah was getting the captain's children ready for bed. The little one, Luke noticed, clung to Sarah much of the time. *The poor things,* he mused, *they've lost both parents in less than a year's time. However, they were adjusting, according to Sarah and the Navis family and the German woman, Gretchen.*

"Vould you like some good strong coffee, Pastor McCabe?" she asked him now.

"Yes, thank you."

Gretchen left the room, but re-entered momentarily, holding a cup and saucer.

"So what will you do, now that you're no longer employed with Captain Sinclair?" Luke asked her, sipping the brew.

Gretchen didn't reply immediately, and Luke thought she intended to ignore his question altogether. But then suddenly she answered. "I think my life is over. Vhat is left for me to do now? Who vould hire an aging housekeeper like me?"

Luke grinned. "Well, pardon my boldness, ma'am, but we sure could use you out West. I know plenty of ranchers who would pay dearly for your housekeeping services. Our little church could use your help, too. We've started a Sunday school and a ladies' Bible study group."

"Out Vest!" Gretchen cried. "I can't move out Vest; I'm almost sixty years old!"

"But you're healthy, aren't you? And Richard told me that you're a believer. Wouldn't you like to be a witness for Christ out in the Arizona territory?"

Gretchen was momentarily pensive. Then she asked, "Are you serious?"

"I am," Luke replied with a smile.

"Then I vill consider your offer. . .seriously."

"Very good, Mrs. Schlyterhaus."

With a curt nod, she turned and walked back into the kitchen, passing Richard on the way. He carried a cup of steaming coffee and, taking a seat across from Luke, he took a drink. An amicable conversation ensued and, within minutes, Marty joined them in his wheel chair. Then Bea strolled in. Then Sarah. Finally Gretchen.

"Tell us about Arizona, Pastor McCabe," Marty requested of him.

Luke grinned. "I was hoping someone would ask!"

"Are there really savages out there? Ready to scalp every man, woman, and child?" Bea asked with wide eyes.

"Yes and no," Luke replied. "First off, I don't think of the Indians as *savages*. They are people, like you and me, and they need Jesus Christ, too. Our government has not been fair with the Indians. That's my personal opinion, of course. And the Indians that I've come in contact with have been anything but savage. On the contrary, they've been very generous, caring, and helpful.

"On the other hand," Luke continued, "some Indians are bitter about their land having been taken from them and it's those tribes that are murdering white folks. That's where the horror stories begin, I'm afraid, and it's a shame it's mostly the bad news about the Indians that people hear."

Murmurs of awe and agreement echoed around the room.

"Well, what about these fellows—these *cowboys* I'm hearing about?" Richard asked. "I've heard that they drive cattle all over creation. . .but for what purpose?"

"For the purpose of feeding the entire western half of this nation," Luke said with a patient smile. "Cattle driving is becoming quite the thing to do lately."

Richard grinned mischievously. "Say, Pops, you and I could do some cattle driving right here."

"Why, sure we could, son," Marty replied with a humorous smirk. "You on your horse and me in my chair."

"Lyla, our fairest Guernsey, leading the way."

They laughed and laughed, while Sarah and Bea exchanged weary glances. Gretchen, however, was chuckling softly from behind her knitting.

Suddenly a voice could be heard, calling from the kitchen. "Sarah? Sarah, would you care to go for a str—"

The young woman with light brown hair stopped short when she got far enough into the house to see the company. "Oh, I do apologize," she said quickly. "I forgot. . .your company. . ."

"That's all right, Beth," Sarah said, rising from her place on the sofa, next to Richard. "Come on in. Let me introduce you to my brother." She turned to him. "Luke, this is Bethany Stafford. She lives on the neighboring farm. Beth, this is my brother, Luke McCabe."

Luke had stood the moment Bethany entered the room. "Miss Stafford," he said politely. "It's a pleasure to meet you."

Bethany seemed to force a tight smile as she curtsied quickly. "Mr. McCabe."

Sarah smiled. "My brother is a preacher out West."

Bethany blushed. "Oh, that's right. I'm sorry. . .pleased to meet you, Pastor McCabe."

Luke smiled graciously. "That's all right, Miss Stafford. You can call me 'mister.' In fact, you can call me anything. . .just don't call me late for supper!"

He chuckled at the glib reply and Richard joined him; however, Sarah sighed and rolled her eyes.

Bethany's blush only deepened. "Well, I have to go, so good night."

"But you just got here, Bethany dear," Bea said as she rose from her chair. "Why don't you stay for a cup of tea?"

"No. . .no thank you. I. . .I think I forgot something at home," she stammered. Then out she went.

Luke smiled in her wake. *She's one shy young lady,* he thought. Then he had an idea that Bethany Stafford might be just the kind of woman who would make a perfect school teacher in the Arizona territory. She was plain enough. The men would leave her alone. . .

"I know what you're thinking, Luke McCabe," his sister said with a little grin.

"And?" he replied with a raised brow.

"And. . .she's qualified, all right." A slow smile curved Sarah's mouth. "And it might be the very thing Bethany needs in her life right now!"

Richard suddenly cleared his throat. "Would you two care to let the rest of us in on this conversation?"

Sarah laughed and then nodded. "Luke thinks he may have found his school teacher for out West. Bethany!"

"Bethany Stafford? Well, sakes alive!" Bea exclaimed.

"Don't you think she'd make a good one?" Sarah asked.

"Teacher? Yes, of course. Out West?" Bea shook her head as if uncertain. "I don't know what her papa would say about all of it, though."

Luke grinned. "Well, I guess I'm going to go visit her papa, then," he said, feeling a purpose growing in his heart.

nineteen

Eight days later, on a lazy Sunday afternoon, Sarah and Richard sat together on the front porch swing. The September day was fair and mild with a light wind rustling through the leaves. Sarah appreciated the colors around her, the fiery reds and rich golds. She breathed deeply of the fresh country air, thinking about so many things. . .

"Do you think she'll take Luke's offer?" Sarah suddenly had to ask, speaking of Bethany.

Richard just shrugged. "We'll know shortly."

Sarah nodded. Luke had gone over to the Staffords' house this afternoon. After days of much prayer, he felt confident in offering the school teacher's position out West to Bethany. . .not Sarah. And what a relief that was for Sarah! At one time, she would have jumped at the chance to go out West with Luke, but now she'd had quite enough of adventure. She had come to realize that she was a simple country girl. . .and that there was nothing wrong with it, either!

"Has Luke decided when he'll take you home?" Richard asked.

Sarah shook her head. "He's concerned about the children. He thinks taking me away could be detrimental, especially since they've lost both their parents in such a short period of time."

"I agree. . .and not just because of personal reasons," Richard replied with an affectionate smile. "Libby and Rachel have been looking to you as children look to their own mother."

"Yes, I know. And I can't say I mind it, either," Sarah said, meeting his smiling eyes. "You know, Luke had thought of taking the children back to St. Louis with us," she confided, "but they're so comfortable here and the children need some stability in their lives. They've got it right here."

"Funny," Richard said pensively as he turned to gaze out toward the orchard, "but that's what the captain wanted for his children all along. . .some stability in their lives."

Sarah nodded. "Yes, that was one of the first things he said to me after I arrived."

Richard shook his head sadly. "Even more amazing is the fact that the captain made no provisions for his orphaned children. Only when they become adults." He took Sarah's hand and held it between both of his. "The captain's will calls for trust accounts to be set up for each child; however, there is no one named their legal guardian. Obviously Captain Sinclair hadn't planned on dying until his children were grown."

"Richard, perhaps he's not really dead," Sarah said hopefully.

He just shrugged. "I suppose it's possible, since his body hasn't surfaced yet. But Lake Michigan doesn't always give up her dead, either. And where could he be all this time if he were still alive?"

Sarah swallowed hard. She would like nothing better than to ignore the entire subject of death, and yet death was very much a part of life. That fact, however, hadn't hit home with Sarah until last month, even with her father and brothers in the ministry. Even after attending dozens of funerals throughout the years. . .except they had all been *Christian* funerals. Sarah had never known an unbeliever who died. But now she did, and she thought it was horribly tragic.

"Wouldn't it be something, though, Richard, if the captain was really alive and well somewhere. . .only we don't know it yet?"

"You're a dreamer, Sarah, that's for sure!"

"Or maybe the captain is alive and well somewhere and he forgot to send a message and tell us!"

Richard laughed. "That would be typical, wouldn't it—the forgetting part, I mean?"

"Yes, it would!"

"But, I must confess," Richard added, "that I'm a little angry with Captain Sinclair for leaving such a mess behind—including that of his children's welfare. His intentions may have been fine for the most part, but the captain was irresponsible in so many other ways."

"Yes, I suppose you're right. He promised the children many things and never followed through on them. Case in point, the children never did get their piano recitals and the party the captain had promised." Sarah fretted over her lower lip momentarily. "I'm afraid to say that and other incidents have caused the children to be somewhat distrustful of adults and their promises."

"A real shame, too, isn't it?"

Sarah nodded.

Several pensive minutes passed as Richard and Sarah both sat there with their thoughts, sorting them through, casting their cares upon the Lord.

"So Luke hasn't said anything one way or another, huh?" Richard asked, moving the conversation back to his original question.

Sarah shook off her musings and smiled. "He did post a letter to my parents on Friday," she told him as her smile broadened. "And I know Luke approves of you, Richard."

"Well, I approve of him, too." He laughed. "We had a grand time at the store on Thursday and Friday. I certainly did appreciate all his help. Luke has practically finished all the inventory. . . in spite of a few pranks."

"You two are a lot alike," Sarah said, pleased but concerned at the same time. To think she wanted to marry someone like her brother Luke!

Richard was chuckling now. "Oh, Sarah! You should have been there last week! You see, the men have been rather slothful since the captain's absence and Luke picked up on it immediately. I, of course, have done the best I can with them; however, they see me as a coworker and not one in position of authority. But Luke. . . Luke implied to the men—without actually lying, mind you— that he had been appointed overseer and that if they didn't quit loafing on the job, they would lose it!"

Sarah grinned. "So what happened?"

"Well, the men didn't take their habitual two-hour lunch breaks on Thursday and Friday."

"Good," Sarah said, feeling that was just. After all, her poor Richard was lucky if he even got a lunch break at all!

"And as far as I'm concerned," Richard continued, "Luke can be in charge for as long as he wants. We're closing up the business and closing up the house, and all the captain's assets will be in probate until he either returns alive and well or the court declares him legally dead. Then, once these matters are all settled, my darling Sarah, I will officially be a farmer!"

Sarah smiled, not minding that latter statement at all. The way she saw it now, she was being courted by the handsomest, most educated farmer in the entire Midwest, maybe even the entire world!

"And if your father allows me to marry you," Richard added, "I believe we're going to be instant parents. . .of four Sinclair children."

Sarah thought it over and then smiled impishly. "Why, I'm going to have four children on the first day that I'm married, while it took poor Ben and Valerie years to produce only three children! Same with my sister, Leah!"

"But you'll have four children in one day?" Richard grinned. "That's quite a feat, Sarah."

"I'll say," she replied with a dramatic sigh. "I'm exhausted just thinking about it!" But truth to tell, Sarah had never relished the thought of leaving those children behind. She loved them like they were her very own already!

Richard was smiling over her last declaration. Dropping her hand, then, he put his arm around her shoulders. "You're quite a lot of fun, you know," he said softly.

"You're not so bad yourself," Sarah replied lightly.

Then Richard's eyes took on a mischievous gleam. "Do you

think your brother would mind terribly if I kiss you?"

"I should say he would!" Sarah exclaimed. "Luke would probably take me home immediately, and I hate to think of what he would do to you."

Richard grinned. "A shotgun wedding, perhaps? I understand those things are quite popular out West."

Sarah rolled her eyes. "Don't get your hopes up now, Richard," she replied on a facetious note.

He just laughed.

❧

Luke McCabe watched with interest as an array of emotions played across Miss Bethany Stafford's young face. Shock at his suggestion that she go out West. Suspicion as to why Luke wanted her to go. Trepidation of facing the unknown. Then, finally, consideration of the whole idea.

As Luke watched, he questioned his initial judgment of her. Bethany wasn't plain at all—not when she smiled, though perhaps she was now, when she frowned so hard. In any case, Luke was prepared to protect her in the Arizona territory where women were a scarcity. He would protect Bethany just as he had been prepared to protect his own sister.

"Well, Pastor McCabe," Mr. Stafford said, rising from his chair, "my wife and I, along with Bethany, of course, will discuss this matter and get back to you."

"Very good," Luke replied, standing to his feet.

"And when do you have to know our decision?" Bethany asked meekly.

"In a week. . .two at the most. If you decide to come West with me, you'll have to buy some supplies and pack. There is, of course, this matter with my sister that I need to settle. I'm waiting for a letter of instruction from my father. I can't leave until I receive it, either. However, I would like to begin my travels back to Arizona before the weather gets bad."

Bethany nodded and gave Luke a timid smile. "I'll pray about it earnestly, Pastor McCabe," she promised. "But I feel in my heart that this would be. . .well, I. . ." Bethany began to blush a pretty pink. "Well, I think I'd like to go."

Luke smiled. "Glad to hear it." Turning to Mr. Stafford now, he said, "And I should add that Mrs. Gretchen Schlyterhaus, the captain's former housekeeper, has decided to travel to Arizona with me. She agreed to act as chaperon for the journey."

With that, Bethany looked at her father expectantly.

"We'll see," he replied, his expression unreadable. He looked back at Luke. "Thank you for the offer, Pastor, and we shall be in touch soon."

Luke nodded and then left the Stafford home.

Walking back through the field to the Navises' home, Luke reflected on Bethany's last reaction to his idea. While her parents seemed skeptical, Bethany appeared to want to go out West. Sarah had said that Bethany had had a couple of heart-breaking experiences recently, and Luke couldn't help but wonder what they were. He also wondered if those experiences were what prompted Bethany's interest in Arizona.

In any case, Luke imagined that Bethany would make a fine school teacher. She had a quiet disposition and didn't seem given to complaining. Furthermore, she seemed patient with children. Being the oldest of her siblings, who ranged in age from four to fifteen, Bethany had helped raise her brothers and sisters. And Bethany was educated. Both Mr. and Mrs. Stafford said they felt education was very important, and Mrs. Stafford taught all her children at home.

Yes, Luke thought now as he reached the Navises' property, *Bethany will make a right proper school teacher! Far more than my baby sister, Sarah—who is hardly a baby anymore!*

Luke's train of thought shifted from Bethany to Sarah now, and he had to admit he found the changes in his sister remarkable. In eighteen months' time Sarah had become a very beautiful young woman. However, the inward changes, emotionally and spiritually, were what impressed Luke the most. Gone was that loftiness and self-assuredness, and in its place was a meek and quiet spirit like the Bible described in First Peter, chapter 3. Luke knew his Bible history well enough to understand that the word "meek" had been translated from the Greek language, meaning "controlled strength." And that's how Sarah seemed to him now. Instead of being overly emotional and effusive, she now possessed "controlled strength." That bit of character, Luke noticed, had very obviously affected the captain's children as well.

Yes, the Lord has done a mighty work in her heart, Luke mused. Then he grinned mischievously. *But she'll always be my baby sister, and I'll always love to tease her!*

ॐ

One week later, Sarah and Bethany stood in the kitchen peeling potatoes for their Sunday dinner. The Staffords were there, as well as Richard's aunt and uncle and Lina and Tim. Everyone was visiting with Luke in the front room, everyone but Sarah and Bethany, that is. They had, out of the kindness of their hearts, volunteered to peel potatoes and help poor Mrs. Navis.

"I love Mrs. Navis dearly," Bethany said now, "but I sure do hate peeling potatoes!"

"I hear you, sister!" Sarah murmured. Then she grinned impishly. "You must admit, though, Beth, it's better to do this task together."

"Are you suggesting that misery loves company?"

Sarah chuckled softly. "Why, yes, I am."

Both young women were smiling as they peeled several more potatoes.

"Your brother preaches a powerful message," Bethany finally ventured to say. "I enjoyed hearing it this morning, and wasn't it nice of Pastor Thomas to let him be our guest speaker?"

Sarah nodded. "I may be partial, Beth, but I think Luke is one of the best preachers I've ever heard—next to my father, of course!"

Bethany smiled. "Speaking of fathers—mine said I could go out West."

"Really?" Sarah stopped peeling in mid-stroke. Then she smiled broadly. "I'm so glad. I think it will be a good experience for you." She paused. "Have you told Luke yet?"

"Not yet. But my father is probably relaying the news to him right now. He said he would." Bethany paused in momentary thought. "Sarah, I think this is the new beginning I've needed. I had been praying. . .for a new. . .well, a new direction in my life. Something to pour my energies into." Bethany smiled. "And here it is: A position as a school teacher. Me! Imagine it! Out West!"

"Oh, I'm so excited for you!" Sarah exclaimed.

Bethany nodded as she picked up another potato. "You know," she began, sounding overly careful, "I fully expected to marry Richard, raise a family, and live right here all my life. I never would have dreamed of leaving Milwaukee. . .or the state of Wisconsin! Yet, here I am, preparing to travel out West with a man who is. . .well, he's. . ."

"He's what?" Sarah demanded, curious what Bethany thought of Luke.

Bethany stuttered momentarily in her reply. Finally she blurted, "Well, he's so. . .so handsome that he makes me nervous!"

"Luke?"

Sarah frowned slightly, feeling a little surprised to hear her brother described that way. *Captain Sinclair, yes. . .but Luke?*

"It's his eyes, I believe," Bethany continued. "They're the eyes of a kind and gentle man, but they can stare holes right through a person, too—especially when he's intent on delivering the gospel."

"Luke?" Sarah shook her head, wondering if they were speaking of the same man. But she realized then that, while Sarah saw her brother as just her irksome older brother, Bethany saw Luke as a preacher and a. . .a man.

"Why, Bethany," Sarah teased her lightly, "I thought you were finished with men."

"Oh, I am!" she declared. "I'm more than finished with men. It's just that. . .well, for a pastor, your brother is, uhm, very pleasing to look at when he's behind the pulpit."

Sarah gasped with pleasure. "Why, Bethany Stafford—and here I thought you were listening to the message this morning!"

"I was!" She blushed and then tried her best at a careless shrug. "I was merely stating an observation, that's all!"

"Well, of course you were." Sarah giggled.

"Now, Sarah, don't you dare misunderstand me. I am really through with men. Getting my heart broken twice is twice too many times! It won't happen again!"

"I should hope not." Sarah paused, thinking everything over. "You know, Beth, I think you just gave your heart away too fast; that's what you did."

"Like I said, it won't happen again." Then she turned toward Sarah. "But I harbor no bitterness toward Richard. . .or you. . .or Lionel. I want you to know that."

Sarah nodded thankfully.

"But I really did love Richard," Bethany confessed in a hushed tone of voice. "I think maybe I still do."

Sarah's heart went out to the girl. "I'm sorry. . .but Richard and I never meant to hurt you."

"I know that. And I also know that Richard loves you and. . .I can see you love him, too."

"Yes, I do," Sarah stated. The more she prayed about marrying Richard, the more she knew it was God's will for her life. "But, you know, Bethany," she added now, "my situation is just the opposite of yours. I never expected to marry a farmer. I wanted to be part of the affluent society, which I have since learned is not all that different from a farming community—not in God's eyes, anyway. We're all people, and people need the saving grace of Jesus Christ. Rich or poor, we all need Him."

"Amen!" Luke declared heartily from the doorway. "Sarah, if

women could be preachers, you'd be a fine one!"

"Oh, quiet!" she retorted.

Luke chuckled.

Sarah then considered him. He was leaning against the wooden door frame with his arms folded across his broad chest. He smiled and his blue eyes twinkled with mischief.

Shaking her head at him, Sarah turned to Bethany. Her friend's face was flushed as bright as Mrs. Navis's roses.

"So how long were you spying on us, Luke McCabe?" Sarah asked with raised brows. She sensed this was the very question on Bethany's mind just now. She was probably fretting over her comment about Luke being handsome.

But Luke just laughed. "I was spying on you only long enough to hear my baby sister say what would be music to our parents' ears. They've wanted to marry you off for a long time now."

Sarah clucked her tongue. "I pity you, Bethany, going out West with the likes of him!" She shot her brother a glance of annoyance; however, glancing over at Bethany, Sarah saw she looked relieved. Luke hadn't heard a word Bethany had said about him.

Luke took hold of one of the wooden kitchen chairs, turned it around, and straddled it, leaning his forearms against its back. "I'm glad you mentioned the West," he said. "Miss Stafford, I guess we're on. Your father gave his permission just minutes ago, and I can't tell you how pleased I am. We need a school teacher in a mighty bad way!"

Bethany nodded, wearing a tight little smile which caused Luke to frown. Sarah knew her brother well and suspected that he was wondering why Bethany didn't appear more excited. The McCabes were an animated family, quite given to their emotions at times. They hugged and kissed each other and didn't think twice about displaying their affections. Bethany's apparent nonchalance would be a puzzle to Luke, of course; however, Sarah wasn't about to divulge the whole of Bethany's secrets. Beth could tell Luke all that she felt he should know. . .

Suddenly she looked from Luke, at her right, to Bethany, on her left, then to Luke again. Something seemed strange—Luke was studying Bethany like he might study an intense chess game, while Bethany, her chin lowered, was peeling potatoes as fast as her hands would go.

There's something between them, Sarah decided, and she felt caught in the cross fire. And then she realized just what that *something* might be. . .

For days, Luke had been asking vague questions about Bethany. Then, today, Bethany said Luke was "handsome," so handsome that he made her nervous.

Can it be? Sarah wondered. She felt like laughing as she looked from one to the other. *Luke and Bethany? On the brink of a romance?*

Sarah shook off her imaginings. What a ridiculous notion. The worst she'd come up with in months!

However, the atmosphere did not lighten until Richard ambled into the kitchen, breaking the spell that seemed to have been cast over Bethany and Luke. Only then did Bethany slow her potato peeling to a comfortable pace.

twenty

Sarah took a deep breath and inhaled the fresh country air. The October sunshine streamed through the autumn-colored leaves above her as she stood in the orchard. Sarah smiled at the beauty surrounding her, and then she resumed her apple picking.

The children, too, were picking apples. Libby and Rachel carried theirs in their aprons; however, the boys were carelessly tossing the apples they collected and occasionally throwing them at each other. But Sarah didn't reprimand them. Gabriel and Michael were just being boys and, as long as they didn't throw apples at the girls—or her—they weren't doing any harm. Mrs. Navis would just have to make applesauce out of what the boys collected today.

"These apples are the last of the crop," Sarah told Libby and Rachel. "But they'll be good in pies, turnovers, and, of course, applesauce." She gave the boys a pointed look.

"I yike apposauce!" Rachel declared, nodding her head vigorously.

Sarah just smiled down fondly at the child.

Suddenly a great noise could be heard coming from the road. Sarah and the children stopped and turned to look. In surprise, they watched as first one wagon—Richard's—and then buggy after buggy pulled into the circle drive. One, two, three, four, five. . .

"Goodness!" Sarah exclaimed. "It looks like a parade!"

The apples were dumped into a large bushel basket which sat on the edge of the orchard. Then Sarah and the children walked toward the driveway to see who. . .or *what* had arrived.

"Mama!" Sarah suddenly cried. Then she saw her father alight from the buggy. "Pa!" She ran to greet them, hugging each parent fiercely.

Much to Sarah's amazement, the next ones out of the buggy were her brother Ben and his wife Valerie, who was holding three-month-old Elaina.

"Why, I haven't even seen this baby yet!" Sarah said, admiring the wee one in Valerie's arms. But then her young nephews, Mark and Joshua, demanded her attention. "Well, just look at you two boys. You sure have grown!"

Leah, Sarah's older sister, suddenly appeared, along with her husband and three children who were near the ages of Gabriel and Michael.

Leah hugged Sarah and then whispered, "I'm expecting a baby myself. After all these years. . .number four!"

Sarah gasped with delight.

Then Aunt Cora and Uncle Marlow emerged from the last two buggies, along with their six children—Cousin Brian being one of them.

"Oh, no, it's you!" Sarah teased him, for they had a long-standing friendly feud going on between them.

"I heard you'd be gettin' hitched," Brain shot right back, "and I came to give your husband-to-be my deepest sympathies."

"Oh, you just hush!"

Cousin Brian laughed heartily and then hugged Sarah so hard she thought her ribs would crack.

The commotion brought Marty and Bea outside. Luke appeared and joined in the welcoming, helping Richard with introductions. Sarah, in turn, introduced the Sinclair children.

"Well, Sarah," said her father, the Reverend Nathanael McCabe, "a letter just wasn't going to suffice. We all had to come in person."

"So I see," she replied, rolling her eyes at Brian.

"And since we're here," Sarah's mother Hannah said, "we thought we may as well have a wedding!"

"Oh, yes, and I even brought my wedding dress for you, Sarah," Leah said with a big smile. "I think it'll fit you just right, too."

Sarah forced a smile, trying to conceal her surprise at the sudden "wedding" plans.

"This is so wonderful!" Bea was saying now. "And how ironic that I was just saying to my sister-in-law Ruth, whose daughter is getting married next week," she explained to Sarah's parents, "why, I was just saying that a double wedding would be so lovely. But I dared not even hope it. . .but here you all are anyway!"

"Next week. . .?" Sarah's head was spinning from all the activity around her. "You can't mean a double wedding with Lina and Tim. . .?"

Bea smiled. "Well, of course I mean a double wedding with Lina and Tim!" She clapped her hands together expectantly. "And all the families together. . .oh, Sarah, this will be so special!"

Sarah nodded, albeit reluctantly. "But. . .next week, already?"

"I reckon next week will be fine," Nathanael stated on a weary note. "But we'll have time to mull things over later. Right now, I feel dead on my feet from traveling."

"Oh, please forgive my bad manners!" Bea told all her guests. "I just get carried away sometimes. Please. . .please come inside."

The McCabe family followed Bea and Marty into the house, Bea pushing her husband's wheel chair, while Sarah turned a troubled look on Richard and mouthed, "Next week. . .?"

He grinned and came toward her, saying, "Tomorrow wouldn't be soon enough for me, Sarah."

"But I can't plan a wedding in a week!" she cried helplessly. "Look how long Lina and Tim have been planning for theirs."

"They were just making sure, Sarah. All that time had nothing to do with wedding plans." Richard gave her a patient smile. "But we're sure so. . .so what's the problem?"

Sarah groped for the words, but could find none to express her tumult of emotions.

Finally Richard cupped her chin, urging her gaze into his. "What's wrong, Sarah?" he asked softly. "You're uncertain?"

The question took her by surprise. "Uncertain?" she repeated. "About what? You? About us?"

Richard nodded.

Smiling, Sarah shook her head. "No, I'm not uncertain about

any of that." She folded her hand into his. "I love you, Richard," she said softly. "I am sure about at least that much."

Just then Melody and Shelene, two of Sarah's young cousins, came out onto the front porch. When they spied Sarah and Richard together, they fell into a fit of giggles which set Sarah's teeth on edge. Then the girls went running back into the house.

"You see, Richard," Sarah began, "it's not you at all. It's my family that I'm uncertain about!"

Richard chuckled. "Well, you can't imagine my shock and surprise when a message arrived at the captain's store, informing me that the McCabe entourage had arrived at Union Depot!"

Sarah grimaced. "My sincere apologies, Richard. I love my family, don't misunderstand me, but there are a lot of them. It's a blessing that only a handful has come."

"There are more coming," Richard told her with a wry grin.

"Oh, dear. . ."

Suddenly Richard called to Gabriel and Michael, "Come help me with this baggage, you boys!" Then, turning back to Sarah, he said, "Don't worry. This will be fun. You'll see."

⁂

Over the course of the next few days, more aunts and uncles arrived, bringing with them cousins and more cousins. The only McCabe that Sarah missed was her brother Jacob, who was still in Arizona. However, those who came were all impressed with the Navises' home and hospitality, and when they learned that Richard owned the farm, they approved of the young man all the more.

"It's the fanciest farm I ever did see!" declared one of Sarah's aunts. "And that young man is the best lookin' farmer around. Why, his fingernails aren't even dirty!"

Sarah was given to blushing over her relatives' remarks on more than one occasion.

The house, itself, was packed full of McCabes. The bunkhouse, too. Finally, Sarah gave Richard her entire savings, which she'd earned as the captain's governess, and asked him to see about some hotel accommodations for her relatives. Richard agreed to do it and even put some of his own cash toward the endeavor.

"I love them, Richard, but I haven't had a moment's peace since they arrived."

"I understand completely." He gave her an affectionate wink and a teasing grin. "Your wish is my command."

Richard returned that very evening with the good news: he had secured an entire floor at the Newhall House, a large hotel on Main Street.

"Mr. Daniel Newhall, the owner, is one of America's largest wheat dealers and he did a lot of business with Captain Sinclair," he explained to the McCabe clan. "Mr. Newhall remembered me as the captain's steward and went out of his way to accommodate us. . .for a very good price, too!"

The McCabes were delighted. They, too, were feeling pinched and cramped; however, they were only too grateful for the Navises' hospitality.

"The hotel is close to the train station," Richard added, "so when it's time for you to leave, you won't be inconvenienced by any lengthy traveling."

The offer was too good to pass up, and all, except for Sarah's immediate family, packed their things and moved downtown. Most had never been in a hotel before. They were simple farming folk who had used all their savings to come to Milwaukee and see Sarah married off. Many had thought they'd never see the day! In any case, Sarah's relatives were of the notion that staying in a big city hotel was something of an adventure and they went away wearing expressions of anticipation.

With the Navis household suddenly much quieter, the parents were able to get properly acquainted. Then, one evening, Nathanael McCabe went for a long walk with Richard, and Sarah knew poor Richard was being drilled, quizzed, and questioned mercilessly. She waited for his return, feeling edgy and only half-listening to her mother and Bea chatting over the hasty wedding plans.

"Are you sure your niece doesn't mind sharing her special day with our Sarah?" Hannah asked. "Now I know I've asked before, but I just want to make certain. . ."

"Oh my, no. Lina doesn't mind a bit. In fact, she's thrilled," Bea said. "Lina and Richard are like siblings, and she's awfully fond of Sarah."

"Well, that's so nice of her. It does make things easier, doesn't it?"

Bea nodded as the conversation turned to flowers and wedding gowns.

"Leah's dress fits Sarah almost perfectly. Just a tuck here and a tuck there. . .I have it hanging upstairs so the wrinkles fall out."

"And I can certainly heat the iron if that's necessary."

"I'm afraid it might just have to be. . ."

Richard and Reverend McCabe returned. Entering the house, Nathanael said sternly, "Sarah, come outside. I'd like a word with you."

"Yes, sir," she replied, getting up from her place at the kitchen table. The mothers watched her go with raised eyebrows, but Richard wore a little grin which Sarah recognized at once. She thought their talk must have gone well.

"Richard Navis is a fine young man," Nathanael finally stated, confirming that which Sarah had already guessed. "He loves the Lord Jesus Christ," her father continued, "and he's certainly crazy about you!"

"Oh, Pa," Sarah said on an embarrassed note. Then she smiled happily. "I can marry him, then?"

"You may." The reverend glanced at his youngest child. "You've grown into a beautiful woman, Sarah," he said. "You could probably marry any man you set your sights on. . .You sure about this one? Marriage is forever, and forever is a mighty long time."

"I know."

Sarah thought about Captain Sinclair and how she had nearly "set her sights" on him. . .or a man like him. But, no, Richard was the one for her. She was certain about that now!

"Can't come home cryin' and sayin' you made a mistake,"

Nathanael drawled.

"I won't," Sarah promised as she smiled at her father's words.

Nathanael grinned. "I know too well that determined little tilt of your chin, young lady. I reckon you're as sure as you'll ever get." Chuckling, he put an arm around his daughter and the two walked back toward the house. "Better promise to visit us at least twice a year," he added, feigning a stern look.

"I promise," Sarah replied. "As long as I'm not in the family way and can't travel," she added thoughtfully.

A broad smile split Reverend McCabe's aging face. His bushy mustache twitched and his blue eyes twinkled. "Well, knock me over with a feather," he said. "It's love for sure! Never heard you talk about yourself being in the *family way* before! Just the opposite, I'd say!"

He laughed loudly, and Sarah blushed over her father's straight-forwardness.

❧

Finally the day arrived, and Sarah dressed carefully with the help of her mother and Leah. Then, after arriving at the church, she nervously stood with Lina in the small, stuffy room behind the vestibule, each awaiting her cue to make her way down the aisle. As she surveyed Lina, who stood just as stiffly as she did, Sarah thought that, to an on-looker, they would seem like two fragile dress-up dollies—like the kind Sarah used to see in the St. Louis shop windows at Christmastime.

"I'm so glad we didn't do this in the summer heat," Lina sighed with flushed cheeks.

"It is rather close in here, isn't it?" Sarah replied with a smile.

Lina nodded, then grinned sheepishly. "Between the two of us," she said jokingly, "we could heat all of Milwaukee this winter!"

Sarah laughed and smoothed the silk skirt of her ivory gown. "You know, Lina," she finally said, "once we walk down that aisle, our lives will never be the same."

Lina dabbed her hairline with the lace hankie in her gloved hand. "You sound remorseful, Sarah. Are you?"

"Of course not!" she replied confidently. "I'm only. . .well apprehensive, I guess."

"Well, I certainly share that particular feeling with you; however, I know Tim will be good to me. And Richard. . ." Lina lifted a warning brow, "well, he had better be good to you, too, or else he'll have me to contend with!"

Sarah was giggling softly. "That's quite a threat, Lina, but it doesn't fit your attire at all!"

"No, I suppose it doesn't. Here I'm to be a dainty little thing in white, but I'm perspiring like a blacksmith!"

Sarah giggled again and the laughter helped to alleviate those nervous flutters in her stomach.

"Richard said he has arranged for the two of you to stay at the Cross Keys Hotel tonight." Lina sighed, looking envious. "Abraham Lincoln spoke there once, you know. The place is quite famous!"

Sarah smiled. She knew. But she also knew why Richard had chosen that particular hotel. "Richard has a friend working there," Sarah explained, "and this friend has agreed to conceal our identities from my prankster brothers and Cousin Brian." She gave Lina a wide-eyed look. "Can you imagine what might occur if those fun-lovin' country boys ever found out where Richard and I were spending our wedding night?"

"I hate to even think about it," Lina replied with an expression of dread.

"Although, my father has threatened all my cousins, not to mention my brothers. They're to leave me alone tonight."

"And, of course, they will obey."

"Of course," Sarah replied, but she was feeling suddenly skeptical. No doubt those rascals would find some way around her father's instructions.

"Well, not to worry."

"Yes, but you should have seen what they did to my sister Leah!" Sarah said with a pout.

"Now, now, it's out of your hands. Ask the Lord to protect you and Richard, and trust your father to handle the situation."

Sensing Lina was right, Sarah shook off all her concerns, sending up a little prayer. "And what about you?" she asked, changing the subject. "Where will you and Tim spend your wedding night?"

Lina smiled and her cheeks grew bright. "We're just going home . . .to Tim's house, which will be my home, too, after today. It's back to school for me on Monday and back to work for Tim; however, we'll take a little holiday during the Christmas season—a belated honeymoon, of sorts."

The pipe organ began to play, and Sarah and Lina exchanged glances.

"That's our signal, Sarah," Lina said.

Leaving the little dressing room, Sarah and Lina met their fathers in the vestibule. Pastor Thomas had again humbly stepped aside so Luke could do the honors of performing his sister's wedding ceremony, and Lina and Tim were gracious enough to allow Luke to perform theirs also.

With knees shaking, Sarah took her father's elbow and slowly they made their way down the aisle. They carefully followed Lina and her father, Richard's Uncle Jesse.

Turning slightly to her right, Sarah spotted Gretchen and gave her a smile. The older woman smiled back. It seemed that all barriers, all strongholds between them, had been pulled down and now a friendship existed. Gretchen had asked Sarah's forgiveness, acknowledging her prejudice and insecurities which, in turn, had caused her to feel "mean spirited," as Gretchen deemed it. Then she said that when she renewed her commitment to God this past summer, He had showed her the Irish people were the same as the German people—all people with feelings and a need for Him in their lives. Sarah acknowledged, too, that she had learned something of the same lesson. . .

"And it is no accident," Gretchen had said, "that an Irishman is taking me out Vest to begin a new life." Shaking her head in wonder she added, "How grateful I am that you came into my life,

Sarah McCabe."

Then last night, Gretchen had given Sarah the pearl necklace which she had worn on her wedding day years and years ago. With tears in her eyes, Sarah had accepted the treasure and, as she thought about it now, she touched with gloved fingertips those same pearls around her neck.

Sarah looked forward again. Near the altar stood Tim on the one side and Richard on the other. Sarah marveled at how handsome Richard looked. She smiled and he smiled back, and Sarah wondered if he was as nervous inside as she was. . .

The ceremony proceeded without incident, much to Sarah's relief. She had expected Cousin Brian to do. . .well, to do *something*. Lina and Tim said their vows first. Then Richard and Sarah said theirs.

Finally, with a jesting smile, Luke whispered, "You have my condolences, Richard, I now pronounce you man and wife." Luke paused then, looking smug. But he didn't move or say another thing.

Finally, Richard said, "Get on with it, man. I want to kiss my wife!"

"Oh, yes, of course. I knew I was forgetting something."

Sarah gave her brother a quelling look.

"By the authority vested in me—"

"C'mon, Luke," Richard hissed, though he was grinning from ear to ear at the prank.

"I now pronounce you man and wife and. . ." Luke smiled. "And you may kiss the bride."

"About time," Richard muttered.

Sarah was smarting from her brother's teasing; however, when Richard took her into his arms, she forgot everything but the warm touch of his lips against hers.

"You're mine, Sarah McCabe—I mean, Sarah Navis," Richard whispered as he pulled away slightly. Then he kissed her thoroughly once again.

And, from the McCabe family, a heartfelt "Amen!" was heard as it echoed through the little country church.

A Letter To Our Readers

Dear Reader:

In order that we might better contribute to your reading enjoyment, we would appreciate your taking a few minutes to respond to the following questions. When completed, please return to the following:

Rebecca Germany, Managing Editor
Heartsong Presents
P.O. Box 719
Uhrichsville, Ohio 44683

1. Did you enjoy reading *An Uncertain Heart*?
   ❑ Very much. I would like to see more books
      by this author!
   ❑ Moderately
      I would have enjoyed it more if _____
      _____

2. Are you a member of **Heartsong Presents**? ❑Yes ❑No
   If no, where did you purchase this book?_____
   _____

3. What influenced your decision to purchase this
   book? (Check those that apply.)

   ❑ Cover   ❑ Back cover copy

   ❑ Title   ❑ Friends

   ❑ Publicity   ❑ Other_____

4. How would you rate, on a scale from 1 (poor) to 5
   (superior), the cover design?_____

5. On a scale from 1 (poor) to 10 (superior), please rate the following elements.

    ___Heroine   ___Plot

    ___Hero   ___Inspirational theme

    ___Setting   ___Secondary characters

6. What settings would you like to see covered in **Heartsong Presents** books?_____

_____

_____

7. What are some inspirational themes you would like to see treated in future books?_____

_____

_____

8. Would you be interested in reading other **Heartsong Presents** titles?   ❏ Yes   ❏ No

9. Please check your age range:
    ❏ Under 18   ❏ 18-24   ❏ 25-34
    ❏ 35-45   ❏ 46-55   ❏ Over 55

10. How many hours per week do you read? _____

Name _____

Occupation _____

Address _____

City_____ State_____ Zip _____

Heartsong Presents Classics!

We have put together a collection of some of the most popular **Heartsong Presents** titles in two value-priced volumes. Favorite titles from our first year of publication, no longer published in single volumes, are now available in our new *Inspirational Romance Readers.*

___**Historical Collection #1** includes: *A Torch for Trinity* by Colleen L. Reece; *Whispers on the Wind* by Maryn Langer; *Cottonwood Dreams* by Norene Morris; and *A Place to Belong* by Tracie J. Peterson (originally written under the pen name Janelle Jamison).

___**Contemporary Collection #1** inclues: *Heartstrings* by Irene B. Brand; *Restore the Joy* by Sara Mitchell; *Passage of the Heart* by Kjersti Hoff Baez; and *A Matter of Choice* by Susannah Hayden.

Each collection is $4.97 each plus $1.00 for shipping and handling. Buy both collections for $8.99 plus $1.00 for shipping and handling.

······ Hearts♥ng ······

HISTORICAL ROMANCE IS CHEAPER BY THE DOZEN!

Any 12 *Heartsong Presents* titles for only $26.95 **

** plus $1.00 shipping and handling per order and sales tax where applicable.

Buy any assortment of twelve *Heartsong Presents* titles and save 25% off of the already discounted price of $2.95 each!

HEARTSONG PRESENTS TITLES AVAILABLE NOW:

(If ordering from this page, please remember to include it with the order form.)

·········Presents·········

Heartsng Presents
Love Stories Are Rated G!

That's for godly, gratifying, and of course, great! If you love a thrilling love story, but don't appreciate the sordidness of some popular paperback romances, **Heartsong Presents** is for you. In fact, **Heartsong Presents** is the *only inspirational romance book club*, the only one featuring love stories where Christian faith is the primary ingredient in a marriage relationship.

Sign up today to receive your first set of four, never before published Christian romances. Send no money now; you will receive a bill with the first shipment. You may cancel at any time without obligation, and if you aren't completely satisfied with any selection, you may return the books for an immediate refund!

Imagine. . .four new romances every four weeks—two historical, two contemporary—with men and women like you who long to meet the one God has chosen as the love of their lives. . .all for the low price of $9.97 postpaid.

To join, simply complete the coupon below and mail to the address provided. **Heartsong Presents** romances are rated G for another reason: They'll arrive *Godspeed!*